My China Story

Fascinations of Modern China

第三只眼看中国

发现中国之美

王新玲 主编

SinolinguA
华语教学出版社

First Edition 2021
Second Printing 2022

ISBN 978-7-5138-2081-3

Published by Sinolingua Co., Ltd
24 Baiwanzhuang Street, Beijing 100037, China
Tel: (86)10-68320585, 68997826
Fax: (86)10-68997826, 68326333
http://www.sinolingua.com.cn
E-mail: hyjx@sinolingua.com.cn
Facebook: www.facebook.com/sinolingua
Printed by Beijing Hucais Culture Communication Co., Ltd.

Printed in the People's Republic of China

PREFACE

In recent years, platforms and services featuring short videos are trending across the globe. More and more international friends pick up their mobile phones and video cameras to record their lives, travels, and work experience in China. They have become narrators of their own Chinese stories and ambassadors of friendly exchanges between China and other countries. Some are engaged in international trade, especially key projects associated with the "Belt and Road Initiative", contributing their wisdom to international economic cooperation. Some have ventured to the rural areas and are helping farmers out of poverty; some work in the sports industry in China, creating new glories in their games; some are dedicated to research in science and the humanities; and some are engaged in the media. Though they come from different countries, they are making great contributions everywhere in China.

Through their lenses, these foreign friends present their unique perspectives of China, telling stories of the country's development, of shaking off poverty and achieving moderate prosperity, of creating new hopes despite adversities, and of interactions with the rest of the world. These stories show their understanding and care for contemporary China, its people, and the changes taking place in the country, explaining their thoughts on China's reform and development, and showing the growing optimism of the Chinese people.

The "My China Story" book series is based on the prize-winning works of the Global Short Video Contest of the same name and features rich images with intriguing stories that are representative of Chinese culture and entertaining to overseas readers. But even more interesting is seeing how people from all over the world who have discovered a new purpose in China are not so different from those of ordinary Chinese people. The books show us that we all share the same desire to pursue our dreams, no matter where we come from.

The books recount the rich, diverse experiences of short video creators in China as they try local Chinese food, visit scenic and historic spots, witness local residents' lives, and enjoy the conveniences brought about by smart technologies. But it also shows a deeper view, offering first-hand experiences of personal contacts between the East and West, tradition and modernity, and the cultural collisions that sometimes occur. Living their lives as the locals, these authors present the rapid development taking place in the country's urban and rural regions, as well as in various trades and professions. They have deep relationships with their Chinese counterparts and use their cameras to reflect the optimism, generosity, and kindness of equally ordinary Chinese from all walks of life.

Each author has faithfully recorded his or her own story, giving readers a true profile of China through an authentic and objective account. To learn more about a country, the best way is to come and see it for yourself and to walk the streets in person. After working and living here for a period of time as these video creators have, perhaps you, too, will find something fascinating in this mysterious, ancient, and yet modern country.

前言

近两年来，短视频平台在全世界范围内火热兴起，越来越多的外国友人拿起手机和摄像机记录在中国的日常见闻、旅行趣事、工作心得，成为了中国故事的讲述者、中外友好交流的践行者：他们有的活跃在中外贸易领域，尤其是“一带一路”沿线重点工程，为中外经济合作付出智慧；有的扎根农村，为中国农村脱贫致富贡献力量；有的化身体育大使，在中国的赛场上重铸辉煌；有的从事科技和人文研究；有的从事媒体行业；有的从事文学创作……他们来自不同国家，活跃在中国的各个行业。

这些外国人通过手中的镜头展现出看中国的独特视角和新奇视点，讲述了他们眼中的中国发展、脱贫奔小康、在艰难中创造生活的希望，以及与世界交往的时代故事，表达了他们心中对当代中国人与中国事的认知和看法，诠释了世界各国人民对中国改革发展和中国人民乐观向上心态的理解和思考。

“第三只眼看中国”系列丛书基于“第三只眼看中国”全球短视频大赛获奖作品编写而成，故事性强，图片丰富，具有极高的可读性和趣味性。丛书汇聚了全球短视频创作者的力量，把海外受众关注的，能够代表中国文化特色的，能够体现中国与世界共同、共通之处的故事传播出去，对于推动人文交流、增进民心相通、促进文化传播具有重要意义。

本书记录了短视频创作者们在中国多姿多彩、妙趣横生的生活，他们除了品尝美食，游览名胜，感受民生，体验智能生活带来的诸多便利，更亲身体会到了东方和西方、传统与现代之间的文化碰撞。创作者们化身为普通老百姓在中国生活，专注于在中国发展自己的事业。他们扎根于中国，通过自己的故事来反映20多年来中国的城市农村、各行各业的快速发展；他们与普通中国人建立起深厚的友谊，通过镜头勾勒出中国老百姓乐观、豁达、和善的民族性格和气质形象。

本书的每位作者都忠实记录了自己在中国的故事，客观、真实地为外国读者提供了一个又一个了解中国的侧面。如果你想了解更立体、更直观的中国，最好的方式就是亲自来中国看一看、走一走，工作和生活上一段时间，也许你从此就会爱上这个神秘的国度。

目录 | CONTENTS

南锣鼓巷里的“洋老板”

A Store Owner on South Luogu Lane

A Store Owner on South Luogu Lane

On the bustling South Luogu Lane (also known as Nanluoguxiang), a shop's name is particularly eye-catching and inviting: "Plastered 8" is shining brightly. When you get into the store, you will see a tall bald foreigner wearing a creative T-shirt that can be seen everywhere in the store. He is Dominic Johnson-Hill, the owner of "Plastered 8".

At the age of 17, Dominic left his hometown in England to pursue a free life and travel around the world. He lived in Africa for a while, then went to South America, then to India, and finally arrived in China at the age of 20. "I am not a big planner. It all happened in a beautiful accident." Dominic says, "When I arrived in China, the economy has just opened up. Everything was just starting to develop; there were so many opportunities. It was a good place to do business. So I chose to stay."

When he first arrived in Beijing, Dominic did not have much money, and he had to hunt around to make money. "At that time, there was almost no

'foreigner' in Beijing, and so foreigners were very popular, and there were many job opportunities," recalls Dominic. "I taught English at companies at one time, then ran a company that did market research. Later, I learned Chinese and some Beijing dialect and began to know some good friends and understand Beijing's history and culture."

In 2003, Dominic met a Canadian girl, his wife, Laura. They moved to South Luogu Lane, rented a store to start a business with their own fashion brand "Plastered 8". The brand name has three meanings: First, plaster; Second, paste things, which indicates Dominic's business is to "paste" creative patterns on T-shirts. He often says, "I am not a painter. I sell creativity. T-shirts are the carrier of my creativity." It also means "drunk as a skunk", which, he says, fits his love for beer. He also likes the number 8 because 8 represents good luck in Chinese culture. He hopes good luck in business, so he named it "Plastered 8".

The T-shirts sold in Dominic's store are all designed by himself. "I like the old objects in Beijing very much," Dominic says. "I go to the second-hand markets in Beijing every week. You can pick out something which is decades or even a hundred years old. These old objects are like windows, showing me the long history of Beijing and letting me know more about the interesting past. They all inspire me."

On the T-shirts sold in Dominic's shop, you can see many exciting and familiar objects: food tickets, subway tickets, white enamel mugs,

washbasins, and so on. These patterns with Chinese historical imprints, even some modern bill stickers, slogans, such as "certificates help" and "medicine collection", have become creative patterns on the T-shirts. "My neighbor, Auntie Kang, once threw an old thermos. I took a picture of it, and we made it into a design." Dominic said with a smile, "My neighbor once said something like 哪凉快哪待着 (stay where you feel cool). I thought it was interesting, and I put it on a shirt." These objects are familiar for Chinese people, but from a foreigner's eye, they are very new. "For me, these objects are quite fresh, interesting, and I put them on my shirts."

Plastered 8 T-shirts drew inspiration from Chinese culture and set off a nostalgic fashion trend. With his unique creativity, Dominic created the Plastered 8 brand, which had developed into a Chinese streetwear brand. By 2009, the Plastered 8 had expanded to three stores in Beijing and six in China. Their T-shirts have been exported to the United States, Britain, France, Singapore, and other international markets. Local or foreign stars wearing Plastered 8 T-shirts can be seen all over the world. Accordingly, Dominic won the "Entrepreneur of the Year" Award in the "2008 British Business Awards".

Besides the brand Plastered 8 he founded, the most important reason for him to stay in Beijing and live in hutong for these years is his special love for hutong culture. “When I arrived in Beijing, there were only about 10 million people. And now it grew to 20 million people. It puts a massive pressure on the infrastructure of an old city. And the city has to develop. Part of the city had to be destroyed to make way for a new economy to make a better life for people. So part of the old city has to be destroyed. It is very sad. What I want to see is that the remains of this old city, like this area, especially places like Nanluoguxiang (South Luogu Lane), can be protected.”

Speaking of this, Dominic sighs with emotion, “Although I don't read many books and don't know the history of the Beijing hutong, in particular, the hutongs are the soul of the city, and it has old history. Many things may not be seen in museums, but still exist in Beijing's hutongs. If you want your children to know more about the history of Beijing, take them to the hutongs more often.” What Dominic does not want to see is that South Luogu Lane becomes a bar street like Houhai. He worked with people from the street office to organize a “creative market” in the lane, which attracted many tourists. Today, South Luogu Lane has become a creative street, as Dominic most wants to see.

“I have lived here for 22 years. I am part of the city. I own a house here. I own a business here. My children were born here. I met my wife here. I absolutely love my life here. ” Dominic says with a smile, “I couldn't be happier. We share a courtyard with other families. My children grow up with neighbors' children. There are so many good neighbors around. I have my own shops. There is hutong culture. I like the feeling that people are familiar with each other, care about each other, and are very cordial. I love Beijing!”

南锣鼓巷里的“洋老板”

走进熙来攘往的南锣鼓巷，有一家商铺的店名特别吸人眼球，让人想一探究竟：“创可贴8”几个字闪烁着醒目的光芒。走进店里，你会看到一位身材高大的光头老外，穿着店里随处可见的创意文化T恤。他就是“创可贴8”的洋老板——江森海（Dominic Johnson-Hill）。

17岁那年，从小在英格兰长大的江森海为追求自由自在的生活离开家乡，开始漫游世界。他在非洲生活了一段时间，后来去了南美洲，之后又辗转到印度，终于在20岁那一年来到了中国。“我不是一个有明确

目标或者计划的人，但这一次和中国的美好邂逅，让我决定留下来。”江森海说，“我刚来中国的时候，中国正在火热地开辟着经济发展的新天地，我在中国随处可以感受到蓬勃的商机，我觉得这非常适合创业，所以我要留下来。”

刚到北京的时候，江森海的身上没有多少钱，他也曾四处打工赚钱。“当时的北京几乎没什么‘洋北漂’，外国人很吃香，工作机会也很多。”江森海回忆说，“我曾去公司教人学英语，也自己开公司做过市场调查。后来我学会了中文和一些北京话，开始认识了一些好朋友，也开始慢慢了解北京的历史和文化。”

2003年，江森海认识了一位加拿大女孩儿——他的妻子劳拉。他们一起搬进了南锣鼓巷，租了一个店面做生意，创立了自己的时尚品牌——“创可贴8”。“创可贴”所对应的英文单词plastered有三层含义：一是创可贴；二是“贴东西”——这正好体现了江森海所做的生意——把创意图案“贴”到T恤上。他常说“我不会画画儿，我卖的是创意，

T恤就是我创意的载体”；另外，这个词还有喝到烂醉的意思，他说这也很符合他爱喝啤酒的习惯。他也很喜欢8这个数字，因为8代表着吉利，他希望自己的生意可以大吉大利，因此他把公司命名为“创可贴8”。

江森海的店里售卖的T恤都是他自己的创意作品。“我非常喜欢北京的老玩意儿。”江森海说，“每周我都会去北京的二手市场溜达，在那里可以找到各种有趣的老物件儿，很多都有几十年甚至上百年的历史。这些老物件儿就像一扇扇窗户，为我展现北京悠久的历史，让我了解更多有趣的过去。它们给我的创意设计带来无限的灵感。”

在江森海的店里所售卖的T恤上，你能看到很多有趣又熟悉的物件儿：粮票、纸

质的地铁票、白瓷缸、脸盆，等等。这些具有中国历史印记的图案，甚至是“办证”“收药”等一些具有时代感的小广告、口号等，都可以成为创可贴T恤上的创意图案。“我的邻居康阿姨曾经丢弃了一件她家的老物件儿——一只暖瓶，我看到了立刻拿起相机拍了照，将暖瓶放入我的设计当中。”江森海笑着说，“我的邻居曾经说过一句话——哪凉快哪待着。我觉得很有趣，也把它放入我的T恤作品设计里。”这些对于普通中国人来说非常常见的物品、极其日常的表达，在外国人看来却充满了新奇。“对我来说，这些物品或者话语都是异常美丽的新奇存在，非常新颖有趣，很吸引人，所以我决定在我的T恤上展现出来。”

创可贴8T恤从中国文化元素中汲取灵感，掀起了一股怀旧时尚风潮。江森海以其独特创意创立的“创可贴8”品牌，发展壮大成为了一个真正的中国街头品牌。到2009年，创可贴8T恤已经扩大到了在北京有三家店、中国有六家店的规模。创可贴8T恤还远销美国、英国、法国和新加坡等国际市场。在全世界都可以看到穿着创可贴8T恤的本地或外国明星。江森海也因此荣获“2008年度英国商业大奖”中的“年度企业家奖”。

除了他一手创立的“创可贴8”，这些年让他一心留在北京、住在胡同里的最重要原因还是那一份对于北京胡同文化的特殊热爱。“我刚来北京时，这差不多只有一千万人口，现在北京的人口数已经是那时的两倍多。人口的增长给这座历史悠久的城市带来很大的压力，因为要发展新经济，要为人们提供更好的生活，所以很遗憾北京的部分老城区没有保存下来。我很希望现在留存下来的老城区，特别是像南锣鼓巷这样的地方能够得到合理的保护。”

说到这里，江森海颇有感慨，“虽然我看的书不多，也不是特别了解北京胡同的历史，但我觉得北京的胡同就是北京城的灵魂，是历史的见证，很多东西在博物馆里可能看不到，但在北京的胡同里仍然存在着。如果想让孩子们多了解北京的历史，就多带他们来胡同转转。”江森海最不希望看到的就是南锣鼓

巷变成像后海那样的酒吧街。在他的努力下，他和街道办事处的人一起合作，在南锣鼓巷组织了一个"创意市集"的活动，吸引了很多游客。如今的南锣鼓巷已经成为了一条文化创意街道，这是江森海最想看到的。

"我住在北京这座城市22年了。我感觉自己越来越成为这座城市的一部分。我在这结婚生子，拥有家，拥有事业，我非常享受这里的生活。"江森海微笑着说，"你想象不出我在北京的生活有多么完美，一家人住在大杂院里，孩子们吃百家饭长大，周围有这么多好邻居，有自己的小店，有胡同文化，我就喜欢这种人和人互相熟悉、关心，很亲切的感觉。我爱北京！"

Scan for a Video
創可貼

非洲小哥的“功夫梦”

An African Boy's “Kung Fu Dream”

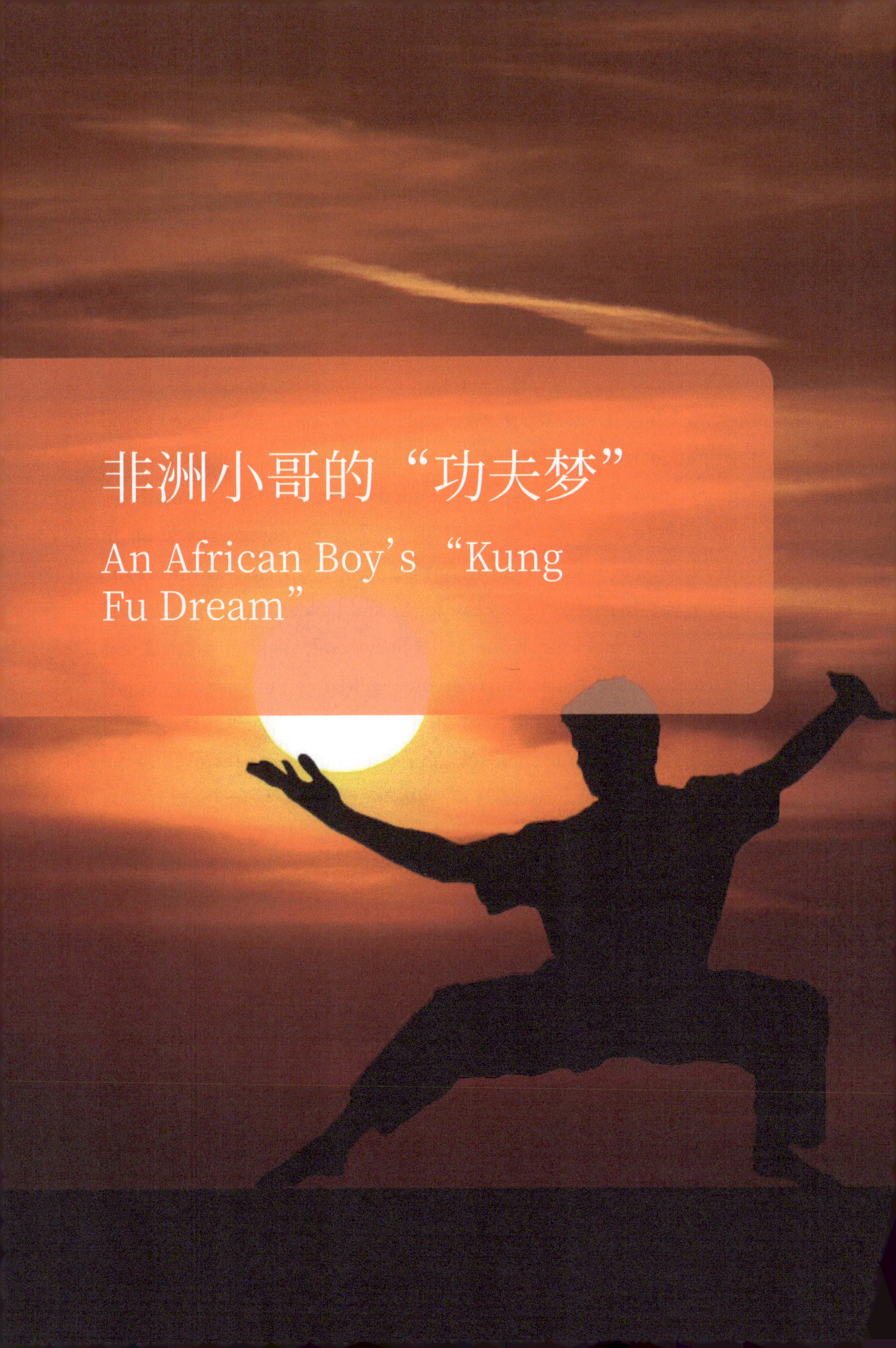

An African Boy's "Kung Fu Dream"

Known as wushu in China and kung fu in the West, Chinese martial arts can be traced back 4,200 years. It has a long history with an extensive and profound tradition. In the ancient dictionary *Shuo Wen Jie Zi (The Origins of Chinese Characters*, compiled in AD 100-121), the two Chinese characters were explained as: *wu* – to be able to stop the fight, martial; *shu* – technique and skill. For several thousand years, Chinese martial arts has been handed down through generations. In the 1960s and 70s, superstar Bruce Lee pioneered the kung fu film genre, and Chinese kung fu became known around the world. Subsequent martial arts stars like Jet Li and Jackie Chan also achieved great success in Hong Kong and Hollywood, making martial arts films even more popular. It has become viewed as a unique, mysterious and fascinating cultural symbol, a virtual window for the world to understand Chinese culture. Kung fu films have inspired many foreigners to travel thousands of miles to come to China and pursue their dream of learning kung fu.

Luc Bendza is from the Gabonese Republic along the western coast of Africa. He came to China in 1983 at age 13 to learn kung fu after watching Bruce Lee and Jackie Chan films. His biggest dream was to be able to "fly around" like the kung fu stars in the films. At that time, he thought that everyone in China knew kung fu and could fly on eaves and walls. When he got off the plane in China, he immediately looked up to the sky for the "flying around" masters. He was confused why he did not see them, and did not know where he should go in order to learn how to fly.

By chance, he was able to visit the Beijing Film Studio just as they were shooting a martial arts film. He saw the actors held by wires, and saw them take flight by hidden people pulling the wires when the director yelled "action". Only then did he realize that the kung fu masters in the films were not really able to "fly around". He was very upset, thinking that Chinese kung fu was a lie, and he even wanted to quit. But this was how he stumbled into martial arts.

For six months from 1984 to 1985, he studied at the famous Shaolin Temple in Dengfeng, Henan Province, the Mecca of Chinese kung fu, where he learned basic skills such as the bow stance, the horse stance, the empty stance and so on. There is a saying that "All martial arts under heaven comes from Shaolin". Shaolin warrior monks regard practicing martial arts as a kind of spiritual cultivation. This period of time in the Shaolin Temple gave Luc a basic understanding of Chinese kung fu, and also strengthened his determination to pursue his dream of learning it. But because he could not speak Chinese he could not continue to learn advanced kung fu. He left the Shaolin Temple to study Chinese at Beijing Language and Culture University. One year later, he was admitted to Beijing Sport University where he majored in martial arts. This is where he got his true education, immersing himself in the study of the traditional spirit, modern theory and philosophy of martial arts. He also learned about the equipment and various fighting styles such as kickboxing, wrestling and other techniques. He began to finally understand what Chinese kung fu really was. For the next twenty years, the boy who once dreamed of "flying around" devoted himself wholeheartedly to learning Chinese martial arts.

Today, Luc is a genuine kung fu master. After learning martial arts for over twenty years, he has come to some deep insights. During the

interview, he shows us the traditional Shaolin fist-palm salute. He raises his hands and makes a fist with his right hand which he places against his left palm which then covers the fist. "The four fingers of the left palm are straight representing virtue, wisdom, physical wellbeing and aesthetics, " he says. "The left thumb is slightly bent inward to imply the humility of man, which warns every warrior to always remain modest instead of being arrogant and proud. The right fist represents strength and rigorous practice. When the fist is covered by the palm, it displays that only when strength is fused with virtue, wisdom, physical wellbeing, aesthetics and humility can it be called martial arts or kung fu." He explains that Chinese martial arts is not only about fighting. It also contains profound Chinese philosophy. It is a way of life. It is like a key that allows a man to integrate himself into society, and also into nature. Wushu uses both martial skills and skills of cultivating one's moral character. They are inseparable. Practitioners should develop their moral character and martial skills, acting out the ethos of martial arts which emphasizes physical wellbeing and moral integrity.

Luc has not only tried to understand the true meaning of martial arts, but has also done his best to put it into action. "The greatest wellbeing for a man is good health," he says. "If you are healthy, you can do a lot of things. Martial arts can build the human body and benefit all of mankind." It is this philosophy which inspired Luc to go back to the Gabonese Republic to introduce martial arts to his country and share the true meaning and benefits of martial arts with the Gabonese people. He set up a martial arts school in his hometown. He says he didn't do this for money, but for his devotion and dedication to Chinese martial arts and also for the benefit of the people of his

hometown. In 1992, he founded the Gabonese Association of Martial Arts. Since then it has grown into an association of more than 1,000 members, making Chinese martial arts well-known throughout Gabon, and even in neighboring countries. Because of him, more and more Gabonese are learning about Chinese martial arts, and even Chinese language and culture. The Gabonese Association of Martial Arts has built a bridge of friendship between China and the Gabonese Republic, has promoted cultural exchanges between the two peoples. It has also helped develop mutual understanding and people-to-people exchanges between the two countries.

In the 38 years since 1982, Luc Bendza has grown from a silly boy dreaming of "flying around" to a true martial artist with a deep understanding and unique view of Chinese martial arts, Chinese culture, and China's social and economic development. "There are many Chinese businesses in Africa, making investments or doing projects, opening factories or running business," he says. "But they have neglected their 'roots', their culture." He thinks that Japan and

South Korea have done well in making karate, judo and taekwondo their cultural icons, and these sports have even become Olympic events. These countries have spared no effort to promote these sports to all parts of the world. Chinese martial arts should do the same. It is a treasure of the Chinese culture, he says, and also an important world cultural heritage. He hopes that Chinese martial arts can also become an Olympic event, and become even more popular around the world. He also hopes that Chinese business people should not focus wholly on making money when they go abroad, and they should also not forget their culture and their "roots".

Luc Bendza, an African man, has realized his "Kung Fu Dream". Now he wishes to introduce Chinese kung fu and Chinese culture to all across the world for the benefit of mankind, which is also the wish of the Chinese people themselves.

非洲小哥的“功夫梦”

中国武术，又叫“功夫”，博大精深，源远流长。中国武术的可考历史已有4200余年。《说文解字》有云：“武，止戈为武；术，思通造化、随通而行为术。”千百年来，中国武术承传有序，延衍繁盛。20世纪六七十年代，一代巨星李小龙开创了“功夫片”的电影类型，中国功夫大放异彩，开始走向世界。随后，李连杰、成龙等一批功夫巨星在香港和好莱坞大获成功，功夫电影风靡全球，中国功夫成为一个独特、神秘、令人神往的文化符号，为世界打开了一扇了解中国文化的窗口。许多外国人看了功夫电影以后有了“功夫梦”，漂洋过海、不远万里来到中国，学习功夫，追逐梦想。

来自加蓬共和国的非洲小哥吕克·本扎就是因为小时候看了很多

李小龙、成龙的功夫电影，萌生了来中国学习功夫的想法，他最大的梦想就是能够像电影里的功夫巨星一样身手矫健，"飞来飞去"。1983年，当时只有13岁的吕克·本扎带着"功夫梦"来到了中国。当时，他以为在中国人人都会中国功夫，个个都能飞檐走壁，所以他一下飞机就抬头看天，寻找那些在天上"飞来飞去"的功夫高手。遗憾的是，他没有找到那些电影中的英雄人物，他也很迷茫，不知道该去哪学"飞"。

一次偶然的机会，吕克·本扎来到了当时的北京电影制片厂，观看了功夫片的拍摄过程。他看到那些演员们身上系着威亚，当导演喊完"action"，后面的人一拉，演员就飞了起来。这时他才明白，原来电影里的功夫高手是这样飞的，并不是真的能"飞来飞去"。他当时很难过，觉得中国功夫是骗人的，甚至不想再练了。但是，没能学会"飞来飞去"的吕克·本扎却无意中闯入了真正的中国功夫之门。

1984到1985年之间，吕克·本扎来到了中国功夫的圣地——河南登封少林寺。他在少林寺学习了差不多六个月，主要学习一些基本功，比如弓步、马步、虚步等。“天下武功出少林”，少林武僧把习武当作一种修行，追求精神的升华。少林寺的练武生涯让吕克•本扎对中国功夫有了基本的体悟和认识，也坚定了他追求“功夫梦”的决心。但是，由于吕克•本扎不会汉语，语言不通，无法继续学习高深的功夫，他不得不离开少林寺，前往北京语言文化大学学习汉语。学了一年汉语以后，他又来到北京体育大学深造，学习武术专业。在这里，他系统地学习了中国武术的传统精神、现代武术的理论知识以及拳术、器械、散打、搏击、摔跤等技能，终于明白了什么是真正的“中国功夫”。其后20年，曾经梦想“飞来飞去”的吕克•本扎把所有的精力都投入到了学习中国武术之中。

现在，吕克•本扎已经成为了一名真正的功夫高手。在练武的20多年中，他更加深入地理解了中国功夫所蕴含的深刻道理。在访谈现场，皮肤黝黑、体格健壮的吕克•本扎兴致勃勃地向我们展示了少林的“抱拳礼"。他抬起双手，左手伸掌，右手抱拳，双手合拢胸前，左手在外，右手在内，松弛有度，微微晃动。他解释说："左手伸掌，四指并拢伸直，表示德、智、体、美；左手大拇指向内弯曲内扣，代表'人'，这告诫每一名武者必须要始终保持谦虚，不自大，不骄傲。右手握拳，拳头代表着力量，表示勇猛习武。左掌掩右拳相抱，意味着只有当力量与德、智、体、美、人融合到一起，才叫武术，才叫功夫。"吕克·本扎明白，中国武术不只是一种搏击技巧，还蕴含着深邃的中国哲学思想，还是一种生活方式，就像一把钥匙，让人把自身与社会、自然的关系融合到一起。武术既是用"武"之术，又是修身养性之术，尚武精神与崇德精神是统一的，武者应内外兼修，德行兼备，追求"修身养性、尚武崇德"之武德精神。

吕克·本扎不仅努力参悟武术

的真谛，还身体力行地把这些思想付诸行动。他说："人最大的幸福是健康，那么有了健康呢，就什么都可以做。武术能让人强身健体，可以造福人类。"于是，吕克·本扎回到了加蓬，他想把武术带回自己的祖国，跟加蓬人民分享武术的真谛和益处。吕克·本扎先在自己的家乡成立了武术学校。他创办武术学校不是为了钱，而是凭借着他对中国武术的热爱和坚忍不拔的精神，致力于中国武术的推广传播和造福家乡人民。1992年，他创办了加蓬武术协会，协会至今已有1000多名会员，使中国武术在加蓬遍地开花，他甚至还把中国武术传播到了周边国家。如今，越来越多的加蓬人开始学习武术，乃至学习汉语和中国文化。加蓬武术协会在中国和加蓬共和国之间架起了一座友谊的桥梁，促进了两国人民的文化交流，推动了两个国家的相互了解和民心互通。

从1982年至今30余年间，吕克·本扎从一个梦想"飞来飞去"的懵懂少年，成长为一位货真价实的武术家，他对中国武术、中国文化，乃至中国的社会和经济发展都有更深的认识和独特的见解。他说："很多中国企业在非洲国家投资、搞建设、开工厂、办企业，但是很多中国人忽略自己的'根'、自己的文化。"他认为，日本、韩国把空手道、柔道、跆拳道打造成自己的国家名片，不遗余力地推广到世界各地，甚至成为了奥运会的比赛项目，中国武术也应该这么做。武术是中国文化的瑰宝，也是重要的世界文化遗产。他希望中国武术也能登上奥运会的赛场，在全世界推广普及。他还呼吁中国企业在国外发展的时候不要只顾赚钱，别忘了自己的文化，别忘了自己的"根"。

吕克·本扎这位非洲小哥实现了自己的"功夫梦"，他希望能把中国功夫与中国文化传播四方，造福人类。其实这也是中国人自己的愿望。

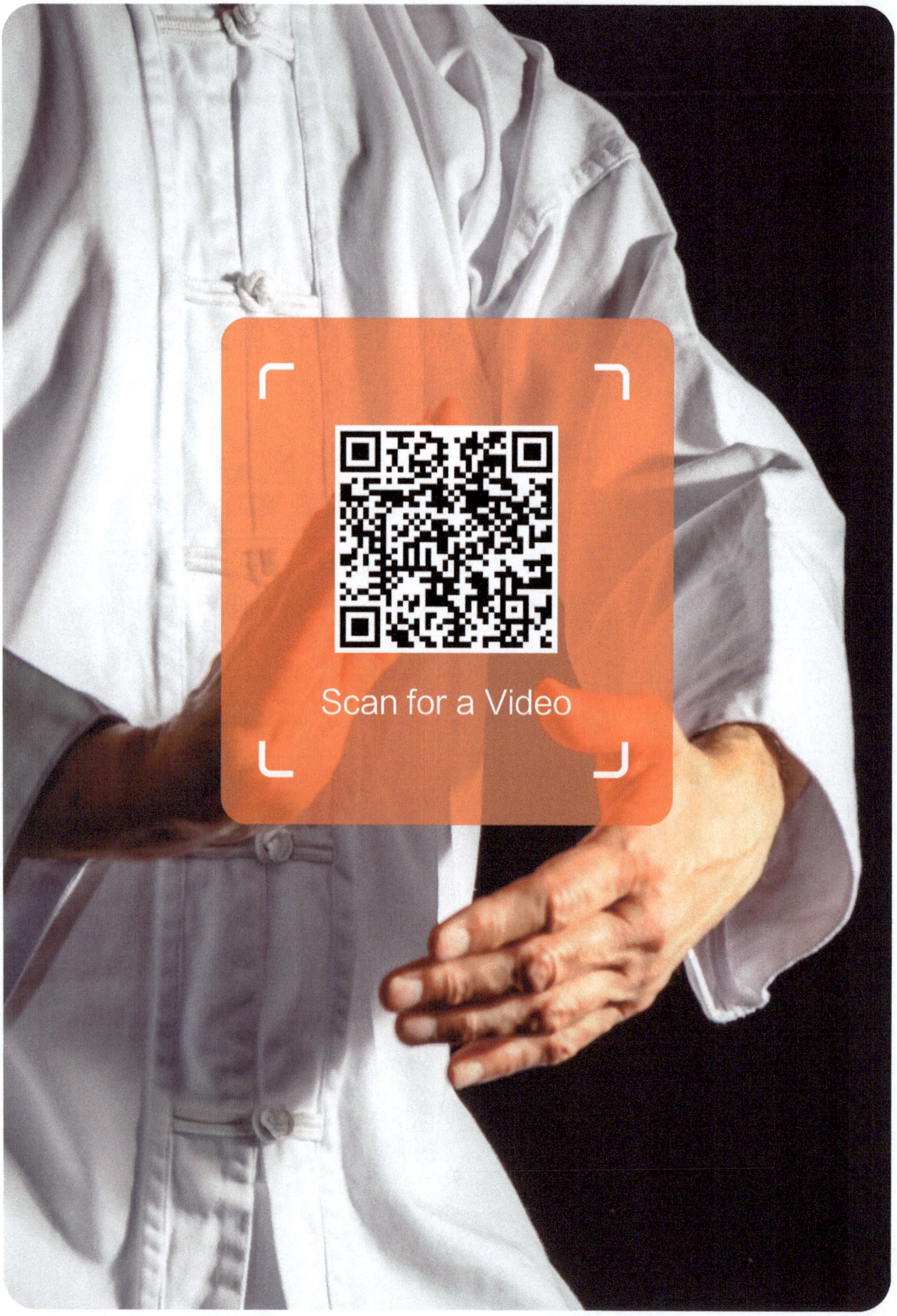
Scan for a Video

老外在北京玩儿摇滚

A Foreign Rocker in Beijing

A Foreign Rocker in Beijing

"There will be overcast skies to heavy snow in Beijing from morning 'til night and snowstorms in the west and north parts of Beijing," says the sweet-voiced weatherwoman on the radio. On the early morning of November 22, 2015, the first heavy snow falls in Beijing. Just after dawn, a tall figure in a red wool hat and a thick overcoat walks out of his home and goes to Gulou West Street. He is Scott MacArthur from New Hampshire in the United States.

"The snow is too heavy today. If I ride my moped, I'll definitely fall and die. It's too dangerous," Scott says, laughing. Scott has blond hair and a strong build, and has been in Beijing for three years. He first came to China in 2009 to study at Peking University which provided him with a rich and colorful learning experience. While at the university, the most unexpected thing happened: he fell in love with music. "It completely changed the course of my life," Scott recalls with

a smile. "After finishing my studies at Peking University, I left Beijing and returned to the United States. But in my heart, I felt that life in the United States was not what I really wanted, so I came back to China in January 2013. I met my bass player, Clancy Lethbridge, and we've been playing music ever since."

We arrived at today's destination: a cramped music rehearsal room on Gulou West Street, and met the members of Scott's band: bass player Clancy, drummer Wang Lei, and acoustic guitar player Shannon Lethbridge. During his three years in Beijing, Scott has created two rock bands, and they play all the time in the bars throughout Beijing. Looking back on these three years, Scott says with deep feeling, "It's not an easy thing to do music in Beijing. You will encounter all kinds of obstacles, especially because we play original music. There is probably not going to be a cover fee and you rarely sell tickets. Even if you do, you'll only make about 100 yuan." Music cannot give him a stable life, but it is his belief that his dream will come true in Beijing. "Music has always had a healing effect on me. No matter what my mood is, I can always find some music to cure me. Music can help me overcome fear, vent my anger and calm my sorrow. Music intoxicates me. I will never give up my music dream." Talking about this, Scott seems to have stars shining in his eyes. "I believe my music dream will come true in Beijing."

Beijing can be regarded as the home base of Chinese rock music. There are countless underground rock bars, mostly gathered in the hutongs of the city center. Some bars are nestled at the back of hutong shops beside grocery stores and video stores... places you can only see at night if you venture near enough. These once-dilapidated spaces have now become trendy music strongholds. The rock music of Beijing's underground bar scene is original and raw, but has strong passion and is full of pure love for music. Scott and his band play in such a bar every night.

"Beijing has 22 million people. How many bands are there? How many different types of music are there? In the past few years in Beijing, I have really seen the Chinese music scene change a lot. In bars around Beijing you will see many bands playing their own original music and style, many styles I have never even heard of. Chinese bands are becoming more experimental and courageous to try new styles and new ideas. Chinese musicians have their own unique, original sound. It's really cool." Regarding the development of Chinese rock music, Cui Jian — the father of Chinese rock music — has to be mentioned. On May 9, 1986, a group of Chinese musicians gathered for a concert inspired by the "One World" movement. Cui Jian, who was wearing a pair of jeans rolled up on one leg, got on stage and roared out the song "Nothing to My Name" at the top of his voice. The song touched not only young people and music fans, but almost all Chinese people, and soon everyone was singing it. After Cui Jian came Black Panther, Tang

Dynasty, Wang Feng, Escape Plan, PK14 and many other rock bands, one after another, bringing a new wave of Chinese rock music.

Under a dim light in the 69 Cafe & Bar, a small, broken, slightly cluttered space located deep in the old Beijing hutong of Nanluoguxiang, Scott and his band are performing their original song "The Drunkard". There are only five people in the audience, but with the sound of the drums and guitars, Scott and his band passionately perform and dance to the rhythm on the stage.

Through his struggle over the past three years, Scott has made numerous like-minded friends in Beijing. They play music together, and encourage and support each other. Scott is growing together with Chinese musicians and Beijing. "I think the future of Chinese rock and roll is really good, and I am very optimistic about China, especially Beijing. I am very excited for the next five to ten years." Scott, full of passion on the stage, smiles shyly, "I love Beijing, the first place I have called home in a long time."

老外在北京玩儿摇滚

“北京今天白天到夜间阴有大雪，在北京的西部和北部等部分地区会有暴雪……”广播里传来气象预报员甜美的声音。2015年11月22日清晨，这是北京这一年的第一场大雪。天刚蒙蒙亮，一个戴着红色毛线帽、全身包裹得严严实实的高大身影走出了家门，往鼓楼西大街走去。他就是我们的主人公——来自美国新罕布什尔州的斯科特·麦克亚瑟。

“今天这雪实在是太大了，还好我是步行出门，如果骑电动车出门，我肯定会摔倒，那我就死定了。这天气太危险了……”斯科特大笑着说。有着一头金发、身材壮硕的斯科特来北京已经有三年了。2009年，他第一次来中国，当时他在北京大学学习。北京大学为他提供了丰富多彩的课程。在学习的过程中，最令他意想不到的是，他在这里开始接触音乐并且真正爱上了音乐。“这可以说彻底改变了我的人生轨迹。”斯科特笑着回忆说，“在北京大学学习结束之后，

我离开了北京回到美国。但在我的内心深处，我一直觉得美国的生活并不是我真正想要的。所以2013年1月我再一次来到中国。那一次回来，我认识了我的贝斯手克兰西（Clancy Lethbridge），从那时起，我们就开始玩儿音乐了。”

正说着，我们到达了今天的目的地，位于鼓楼西大街的一间狭小的音乐排练室，见到了斯科特的乐队成员：贝斯手克兰西、鼓手王磊（音译），木吉他香农（Shannon Lethbridge）。在北京的三年时间里，斯科特组建了两支摇滚乐队，他们一直在北京的酒吧里演出。聊起这三年的经历，斯科特深有感触地说：“在北京做音乐确实不是一件容易的事情，会遇到各种各样的障碍。特别是像我们做原创音乐的，在酒吧演出不会拿到入场费，也很少会卖门票，即使卖也最多只是100块钱。”虽然现阶段音乐并不能带来稳定的生活，但斯科特坚信在北京他可以实现自己的音乐梦想。“音乐对于我来说，总是有治愈的作用。不管心情如何，总能找到一首适合的音乐来治愈我。音乐可以让我战胜恐惧，发泄愤怒，平复悲伤。音乐总能让我沉醉其中，我永远不会放弃我的音乐梦想。”谈起自己的音乐梦想，斯科特的眼里仿佛有无数的星星在闪耀着。“我相信，在北京，我的音乐梦想终会实现的。”

北京，可以算得上是中国摇滚音乐的根据地。这里有无数的地下摇滚酒吧，它们大多聚集在中心城区的胡同里，有的酒吧就窝在小巷子临街店铺的尽头，旁边有各种杂货铺、音像店……大晚

上的，只有走到跟前儿，才能瞅出个“吧”的样子来。这些曾经破旧的空间如今变成人们趋之若鹜的潮流据点。北京地下酒吧的摇滚音乐是原始的，少有修饰，却有着浓烈的热情和对音乐纯粹的、别无其他的爱。斯科特和他的乐队每天晚上就在这样的小酒吧里演出。

“北京有2200万人口，有多少乐队，又有多少音乐种类在迅速扩张？我在北京的这几年，真切地感受到中国的音乐环境改变了很多。在北京大大小小的各种酒吧里，你会看到有很多乐队在演奏着自己的原创音乐，演绎着自己的音乐风格。很多风格甚至是我从未听过、接触过的。中国的乐队越来越有创意，越来越有勇气去尝试新风格、新思路。中国的音乐人有着他们自己独特的、原始的声音。我认为这真的非常酷。”

聊到中国摇滚音乐的发展，就不得不提“中国摇滚音乐之父”——崔健。1986年5月9日，一群中国音乐人聚在一起参加受“四海一家”运动启发而举办的音乐会。当时穿着一只裤腿卷着的牛仔裤登上舞台的崔健，扯开嗓门吼出了那首《一无所有》。那首歌不仅仅感动了年轻人和乐迷，还感动了几乎所有人，在中国几乎人人都能哼唱它。在崔健之后，黑豹乐队、唐朝乐队、汪峰、逃跑计划、PK14等各种风格的摇滚乐队和摇滚人纷纷涌现，带来了中国摇滚音乐的

新浪潮。

昏暗的灯光下，狭小破旧、略显凌乱的空间里，在那一间位于北京老胡同南锣鼓巷深处的69咖啡酒吧内，伴随着斯科特那嘶哑个性的嗓音，他和他的乐队正在演唱着他们2014年的原创歌曲《酒鬼》（The Drunkard）。今天酒吧的观众只有零零散散的五位，但伴随着鼓声和吉他声响起，舞台上的斯科特和他的乐队跟随着节奏舞动，开始了他们激情四射的表演。

这三年来对音乐的不懈坚持，让身处异乡的斯科特在北京结交了无数志同道合的朋友。他们一起玩儿音乐，互相鼓励、互相支撑着。斯科特和中国的音乐人、和北京共同成长着。“我认为中国摇滚音乐的前景真的很好，我很看好中国，尤其是北京。我非常期待未来五至十年中国的发展。”舞台上激情洋溢的斯科特此时却腼腆地笑着，“我爱北京，这是一个很久以来被我称为家的地方。”

Scan for a Video

马布里：为何选择中国？这里就是我的家

China, a Place Marbury Calls Home

China, a Place Marbury Calls Home

He was once one of the most expensive NBA players, being a popular yet controversial All-Star player. His name is known by all basketball fans, especially among Chinese fans. He is the legendary star, Stephon Marbury.

Marbury's NBA career began in 1996. Over his career, he had played for the Timberwolves, the Knicks, the Celtics, and five other teams. At his peak, he could get 50 points in a single game; however, he got the name of "lone wolf" for handling the ball for too long, shooting excessively, and having a bad relationship with other players and teams. His playing time became less, and eventually, he ended his NBA career. His love of basketball brought him across the ocean to China.

Before coming to China, Marbury did not know much about China except Yao Ming and the Great Wall. In this strange country, he needed to adapt to the basketball games and a new life.

First, he joined the Shanxi team, and then transferred to the Foshan team. Marbury did not perform well in these two teams, which aroused the voices of doubt; however, Marbury did not let go of his basketball dream, neither during his peak time in NBA nor when he felt lost in Shanxi and Foshan. He dreamed of playing on the Beijing team. From the first time he arrived here, Marbury considered this possibility. When the opportunity came, he seized it decisively. In 2011, Marbury joined the Beijing team and came to Beijing, China's capital, which he had been longing for.

When he had just joined the team, many people still questioned this former NBA star. But soon after the start of the season, Marbury dispelled these doubts with his performances. In the first 13 games of the season, he led the team to 13 consecutive wins and finally helped the team enter the finals as the second-place team, facing the strongest Guangdong team that year. Marbury was found to have come back to his peak in these games, averaging 33.4 points, 4 rebounds, and 6.2 assists per game, making him the most dazzling star in the CBA. Although he failed to get the finals MVP award, 18,000 people in the audience stood up and shouted "MVP" for Marbury at Wukesong Indoor Stadium after the game, making him the uncrowned king of the whole season.

Marbury cherishes the achievements he made in China. He attributes these achievements to the support of the fans, the coach's guidance, and his teammates' unity.

Marbury says, "There are many people behind us to push us forward to win, such as the Beijing fans. Coach Min Lulei's instruction is certainly more important. And my teammates, they fight hard, always ready to fight. I feel great because this is the championship I won with my teammates. We have a common goal, work hard together, and finally achieve the goal. My goal in life is to win the championship."

For Marbury, knowing no Chinese in an unfamiliar environment was a great challenge. Compared to the championship won in the NBA, the championship in China was obtained after overcoming all the difficulties, which had special significance. Marbury says, "At that time, I was not as familiar as I am with Chinese culture now. It is different from winning the championship in a familiar environment."

During his six years with the Beijing team, he led the team to three championships, won two MVPs, and became the team's soul. Even Min Lulei, the head coach of the Beijing team at that time, said that Marbury revitalized the team, "The Beijing team can do without me, but not without Marbury." At this point, he had come to the peak of his basketball career. People began to nickname him "Lao Ma".

In February 2018, Marbury played his last game in the CBA and announced his retirement, ending his 22-year career as a professional player, but he did not give up basketball. During his stay in China, he set a more ambitious goal in life, using his expertise to contribute to Chinese basketball.

Chances favor the minds that are competent and prepared. After retirement, Marbury soon got the opportunity to coach in the Affiliated High School of Peking University. A year later, Marbury became the head coach of Beijing Royal Fighters in June 2019. Although he liked to guide his teammates in the latter part of his career, even played the role of assistant coach most of the time in the team, it was the first time he acted as a head coach. There is undoubtedly a big difference between a player and a coach. Marbury says happily, "The roles of a player and a coach are completely different, and now I finally got to know that. It's amazing because it shows my progress and change at different stages of life." He is also constantly trying to upgrade himself in the process, hoping to build a championship team culture and stronger competitive spirit for the Beijing Royal Fighters.

When he was a player, Marbury once had the idea of coaching the Chinese national team, but later, he changed his mind. In his view, culture is the crucial element that helps a team compete at a higher level. From a cultural point of view, it is more appropriate for a Chinese coach to be the head coach of the national team, and he can support the head coach as an assistant coach to maximize his value.

Marbury has now become well-acclimated to Chinese culture. From Shanxi to Guangdong, and then from Guangdong to Beijing, every place is different in culture, food, language, and people; each is a new way of life for him. Having lived in Beijing for so many years, he has fallen in love with life in Beijing. He lives in Wangfujing and likes to go jogging with older men and women in the Temple of Heaven. His Chinese is getting better and better. He often goes to Sanlitun to listen to the Deyun Society's cross-talk, even sometimes performs with actor Cao Yunjin. He has many good friends in sports, literary, and artistic circles and has more than 5 million fans on Weibo. Marbury said that China gave him a chance to play basketball and changed his life. In his answer to one of his fans, he sincerely said, "I love living in Beijing. It's not anything different than me living in New York. This is my home."

In 2012, the Beijing Municipal People's Government awarded Marbury the "Great Wall Friendship Award". He is the first foreign player in CBA's history to obtain a permanent residence permit in China, and he is always the "Lao Ma" in the eyes of Chinese fans.

马布里：为何选择中国？这里就是我的家

他曾经是NBA年薪最贵的球员之一，既有全明星球员的光环，也曾饱受争议。提起他的名字，在篮球迷，特别是中国篮球迷当中，无人不知，无人不晓——他就是传奇明星马布里。

马布里的NBA职业生涯开始于1996年。十几年当中，他转战森林狼、尼克斯、凯尔特人等五支球队，参加了无数场比赛，巅峰时期，他单场比赛能拿到50分。可是因为控球时间过长、出手次数过多、跟球员球队不睦让他背上了“独狼”的绰号。他在

球队中上场的时间越来越少，最终结束了他的 NBA 生涯。

对篮球的热爱让他远渡重洋，来到中国。

来中国以前，马布里对中国的了解不多，只知道姚明和长城。在这个陌生的国度里，他需要适应的不仅仅是篮球赛场，更是全新的生活。

他先加盟了山西队，之后又从山西队到了佛山队。在这两支球队中，马布里并没有出色的表现，质疑的声音出现了。可是，在马布里的心中，对于篮球的梦想并没有完全终结，在 NBA 的巅峰时期没有，在山西、佛山失落的时候也没有。他梦想在北京队打球。从第一次来到这里时，马布里就设想过这种可能。当机遇真的到来，他果断地抓住了。2011 年，马布里转会加盟北京队，来到了向往已久的中国首都——北京。

刚刚加盟球队时，还是有很多人质疑这位曾经的 NBA 明星。可是赛季开始不久，马布里就用自己的行动打破了这些质疑。在赛季的前 13 场比赛中，他率领球队取得了 13 连胜，最后以第二名的成绩，一路杀进了

总决赛，正面迎战当年实力最强的广东队。在一系列的比赛之中，人们发现，那个巅峰时期的马布里回来了，平均每场比赛33.4分，4个篮板和6.2次助攻，让他成为CBA赛场上最耀眼的明星。虽然最终没能获得总决赛MVP的殊荣，但是，比赛结束之后，在北京五棵松体育场，18000名观众为马布里起立高喊“MVP”，那无比震撼的场面，让他成为整个赛季真正的无冕之王。

马布里自己也非常看重在中国取得的成绩。他把这些成绩归功于球迷的支持、教练的指导和队友们的团结。

马布里说：“有很多人在背后支持着我们，推动我们前进并取得胜利，例如北京的球迷们。闵鹿蕾教练的指导更是功不可没。

还有我的队友们，他们拼尽全力，时刻准备战斗。我感觉很棒，因为这是我和队友们一起拿下来的冠军。我们有了共同的目标，一起拼搏，最后实现了目标。我的人生目标就是要得冠军。”

除此之外，不懂中文、陌生的环境，对他来说都是巨大的挑战。能够克服种种困难在中国获得冠军，相比于在NBA赛场上获得的冠军，又多了一份更加特别的意义。马布里说：“那时我不像现在这样，对中国文化那么熟悉，这和我在熟悉的环境里夺冠的感觉是不一样的。”

在北京队效力的六年时间里，他带领球队赢得三次总冠军，而他本人也获得了两座MVP，成为球队的灵魂人物。就连当时的北京队主教练闵鹿蕾都说，是马布里盘活了球队，“北京队可以没有我，但不能没有马布里。”至此，这位篮球巨星的球员之路已经走到了巅峰。人们亲切地称呼他“老马”。

2018年2月，马布里打完了在CBA的最后一场比赛，宣布退役，结束了22年的职业球员生涯。但他依然没有放弃一直专注的篮球事业——在中国的这段时间里，他树立了一个更加宏伟的人生目标，他决定用多年的专业经验为中国篮球事业做出贡献。

机遇总是青睐有实力、有准备的人。退役之后，马布里很快获得了在北大附中任教的机会。执教初中男篮队一年后，马布里在2019年6月成为北京北控队主帅。虽然在职业生涯后期他就非常喜欢指导队友，很多时候他都扮演着球队中助理教练的角色，还被人们笑称为“马政委”，但作为主教练，马布里还是第一次。做球员和当教练，当然有很大的不同。马布里开心地说：“当球员和当教练是两种截然不同的感受，而我现在终于都体会到了。这是一件美好的事情，因为这展示了人生不同阶段的进步和改变。”

在这个过程中，他也在不断努力地去建设自己，希望给北控队建立一种冠军球队的文化，拥有更强的竞争精神。

在做球员的日子里，马布里也曾有过执掌中国国家队的想法，但后来他的想法改变了。在他看来，文化至关重要，它是一个球队能够拥有更高层次竞争力的能量。而从文化层面来看，让中国教练来当国家队的主帅更加合适，他自己可以在助理教练的岗位上辅助主教练，发挥自己的价值。

如今的马布里已经融入中国的文化当中了。从山西到广东，又从广东到北京，每到一处，文化、食物、语言、人都不一样，对他来说，都是一种新的生活方式。在北京生活了这么多年，他已经爱上了北京的生活。他住在王府井，喜欢去天坛跟老头儿老太太们一起慢跑。他的中文越来越溜儿，不仅经常去三里屯听德云社的相声，还跟相声演员曹云金一起登台说相声。他有很多体育界、文艺界的好朋友，在微博上的粉丝超过了500万……马布里说："中国不仅给了我一个打篮球的机会，也让我的生活焕然一新。"面对别人的提问，他诚恳地说："我爱北京的生活。我在这里和我住在纽约没有区别，这里就是我的家。"

2012年，北京市政府授予马布里"长城友谊奖"。他是CBA历史上首个获得中国永久居留证的外援，更是中国球迷心目中永远的"老马"。

Scan for a Video

捷克的“齐白石”

The Czech “Qi Baishi”

The Czech "Qi Baishi"

On the campus of the Central Academy of Fine Arts in China, a man with blue eyes, a tall nose, and a brown beard can often be seen riding an old-style bicycle. He often wears a traditional Chinese gown and carries a backpack. He is the Czech artist Jiri Straka, nicknamed "Czech Qi Baishi" after a renowned painter in modern Chinese history.

When speaking of the origin of his nickname, Jiri bursts into laughter and says, "It was between 1978 and 1979. I was in the fifth grade. On the bookshelf of my parents' study, I found a book. It was a collection of paintings by the master painter Qi Baishi. I was absorbed by it. That was when my addiction to traditional Chinese painting began. My classmates joked around by calling me Qi Baishi, because I had the book with me at all times."

From then on, Jiri became very curious about China and began collecting various items related to this country, such as Chinese ballpoint pens, erasers, boxes with Chinese characters on it.... He even asked one of his friends to help buy Chinese brushes from Germany.

"At that time, I was fascinated by China and looking forward to going there to study Chinese painting." When he was about to graduate from middle school, Jiri wanted to apply for a fine arts academy in Czech. At that juncture, the famous Czech Sinologist Mr. Oldrich Kral, whom he met through his friend, gave Jiri a piece of advice: If he wanted to study Chinese painting and gain a deeper understanding of it, he must learn the Chinese language, history, and culture.

Therefore, Jiri chose to study Chinese at the Chinese Department of Charles University. In 1991, he took his first trip to China as a university student. Back then, Beijing was quite different from what it is now, and several months of overseas study left him a deep impression. Jiri says, "At that time, Beijing was quite different from now. There were many bicycle riders on the street, the population was very large. That big city impressed me a lot." In 1995, upon his graduation from the Chinese Department of Charles University, Jiri got closer to his dream as he was admitted to the Central Academy of Fine Arts in China to study traditional Chinese painting. He believed that only in China could he access the essence of Chinese ink painting. At the start of his study, Jiri was very interested in the traditional painting materials, such as Xuan paper, brushes, ink, and mineral pigments. He often pondered: How can other people depict their subjects on paper so freely and naturally? He kept painting plum blossoms, orchids, bamboo, and chrysanthemums as well as the traditional flower and bird themes.

After graduating from the Central Academy of Fine Arts, Jiri returned to the Czech Republic and worked at the Asian Section of the National Gallery of the Czech Republic, where he studied Chinese painting and did some repair work for the paintings. However, the life in his home country wasn't so good as he had expected. Jiri felt that his dream of becoming a wash painting master was becoming more elusive. At that time, the National Gallery of the Czech Republic just had a new curator, which led to the cancellation of all his projects. Worse still, the painting materials like the Chinese Xuan paper were becoming hard to come by. On the other hand, Jiri also entered a bottleneck period in Chinese painting creation. This tormented him. He said, "Chinese ink painting is closely knit with Chinese history and culture. Over the course of several thousand years, it has taken in many key components of Chinese civilization. It has rich connotations, which

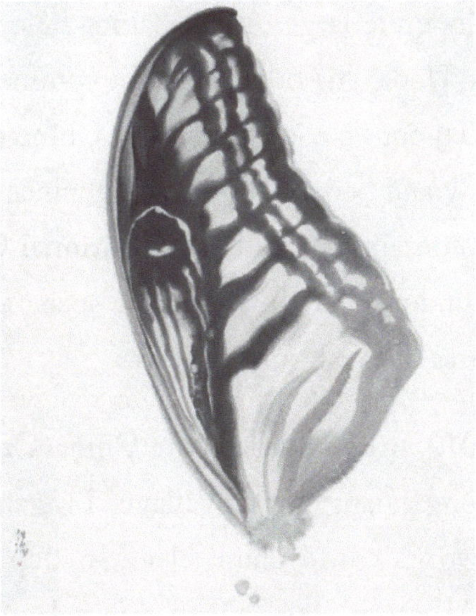

is sometimes hard to find in Europe. I felt a bit lonely. When I was back home, Chinese society was undergoing huge and incredible changes. This was a very special environment, inspiring me from different angles. I think this was very important, and this is why I wanted to work in China."

After returning to China, Jiri gradually found his own values in his works amid the drastic changes of the Chinese society. His attitude and understanding regarding art creation have changed as well. He started to paint something of his own. In his words, he found a language that belonged to himself, through which he could express his viewpoints on existence. Jiri could not find any inspiration in painting back home. But after he returned to China, everything around him seemed to be so familiar. Even a small everyday item could be inspirational and hence became part of his work. Instead of following the freehand style which has been the mainstream of ink-and-wash painting, he often knelt down on a piece of paper to paint the real mountains, rivers, flowers, and plants in front of his eyes. The size of his paintings is usually quite large. As he paints, he often uses a hair drier to dry the work. Under his brush, a lot of common things, such as a fly, goldfish, feather, popsicle, clothing, and Chinese cabbage, have been magnified greatly and become important themes of his paintings. His works not only contain the traits of traditional Chinese wash painting, but are also endowed with a sense of space and vividness that are common features of Western paintings.

In 2010, Jiri established the China-Czech Contemporary Art Gallery in Songzhuang Artist Village, Tongzhou District, Beijing. He hopes his works could channel an in-depth dialogue between Chinese and Western arts. "Deep down I am still a Westerner. I received Western sketch training, and I like ancient European and Baroque style paintings. But I have had an affinity for Chinese paintings since childhood. I have even accepted some Chinese ways of thinking in my life. It made me feel so painful at the very beginning. To me, these two civilizations were just like a cocoon that always bound me up. I often wondered: What should I do? Subsequently, I came up with an ideal and interesting way. I hope my works could present traditional Chinese culture and be combined with traditional Chinese elements, and at the same time, show the influence of traditional Western schools of arts, such as Baroque. For me, each work is a dialogue between two different civilizations."

Jiri is just like the catfish in the field of Chinese ink-and-wash art. He has blazed a new trail in Chinese wash painting and succeeded in integrating Chinese and Western cultures which are quite different from each other. Jiri says that he will continue his work in China, and the story of the "Czech Qi Baishi" is still unfolding in this country.

捷克的“齐白石”

在中国中央美术学院的校园里，你时常可以看到一位蓝眼睛、留着金黄头发和褐色胡须，穿着中国传统大褂，背着双肩包，骑着老式自行车的外国人。他就是被称为“捷克齐白石”的捷克艺术家伊瑞（Jiri Straka）。

说起这个称呼的由来，伊瑞不由得哈哈大笑起来。“在我小学五年级的时候，大概是1978、1979年，我在父母书房的书架上偶然发现了一本书，那是一本齐白石的画册。我还记得当时我特别的激动，我被画册里的那些画深深地吸引了，我觉得那些画非

常神奇，非常漂亮。看到它们，我觉得很震撼。从那以后，我开始疯狂地迷恋上中国绘画，无论走到哪里，我身上都一直带着那本齐白石画册。我当时的同学就开玩笑，叫我‘齐白石’。”

从那时起，伊瑞就对中国充满了好奇，他开始收集一切和中国有关的东西，比如文具店里卖的中国圆珠笔、橡皮，还有带汉字的盒子，等等。他甚至还托朋友帮他从德国买回了中国的毛笔。“那个时候我就对中国充满了向往，期待将来某一天可以去中国学习中国的绘画。”中学快毕业的时候，伊瑞想考捷克的美术学院，那时，他通过朋友辗转认识的一位捷克著名汉学家——卡耐尔先生建议他，如果他想学习中国绘画，想对中国的绘画多一些深刻的理解，他就必须去学中文，去了解中国的历史和文化。

于是，伊瑞选择了在查理大学中文系学习中文。1991年，在查理大学读中文系的伊瑞第一次来到中国。那时候的北京和现在完全不同，几个月的留学生活给伊瑞留下了深刻的印象。伊瑞说：“那个时候的北京是完全不一样的，街上都是自行车，人特别多，那个巨大的城市给我印象很深。"1995年，伊瑞在查理大学中文系毕业之后，终于如愿以偿来到北京的中央美术学院学习国画。他认为，只有在中国才能真正学到水墨画的精髓。刚开始学习的时候，伊瑞对中国画的绘画材料，如宣纸、毛笔、墨及一些矿物原料很有兴趣。他总是在琢磨一个问题：别人是如何很自由地、很自然地将这些日常所见在画纸上展现出来的呢？他一直不断地练习画

梅兰竹菊、传统的花鸟。

从中央美术学院毕业以后，伊瑞回到了捷克，在捷克国家美术馆亚洲馆工作，研究中国绘画，也进行一些中国画的修复。但是，在捷克的生活并不如伊瑞想象的那般美好，他感觉自己距离成为水墨画大师的梦想越来越遥远了。当时捷克国家美术馆换了馆长，伊瑞所有的计划都被取消了，甚至后来连想要得到一些作画的材料，例如中国的宣纸等都变得很困难。另一方面，伊瑞当时的国画创作也进入了瓶颈期，这令他很痛苦。“水墨画和中国的历史、文化有着十分密切的关系，几千年来，它吸收很多中国文明重要的东西，因此水墨画的内涵特别的丰富。我觉得在欧洲还是缺乏这样的文化气氛，我觉得有点儿孤独。我回来的那段时间，中国社会正面临着巨大的、不可思议的变化，这是一个很特殊的社会环境，给了我很多灵感。我觉得这对于绘画创作来说是最重要的，因此我决定在中国进行我的水墨画创作。”

回到中国以后的伊瑞，随着中国社会的巨大转变，也渐渐在创作中找到了自我。他

开始慢慢改变自己对创作的态度和理解，开始画属于自己的东西。用他的话说，就是完全找到一种自己的语言，一种表达自我存在的语言。在捷克，伊瑞没有任何绘画的灵感，但来到中国以后，中国的一切对他来说都特别有亲切感，就算是一个日常生活中的小物件也能带给他灵感，成为他的创作对象。他在绘画手法上没有延续中国主流水墨画的写意文人画风，而是直接面对真实的山水和花草植物，跪在纸上创作。他的画尺幅通常很大，边画边用吹风机吹干画面。许多生活中常见的事物，例如苍蝇、金鱼、羽毛、雪糕棒、衣物、白菜等，都被伊瑞放大到惊人的尺度，成为他绘画中的重要题材。他的作品

既有中国水墨画的墨趣，又被赋予传统西画的空间感和造型生动感。

2010年，伊瑞在北京通州的宋庄创建了中捷当代美术馆，他希望自己的作品能实现中西方不同创作理念间的完美对话。“我觉得自己骨子里仍是一个西方人，我接受过西方素描的培训，喜欢古代的欧洲绘画，喜欢巴洛克式的绘画，但是我从小最热爱中国绘画，甚至在生活上我都接受了很多中国的理念。一开始，这让我很痛苦，这两种文化对于我来说就像一颗茧，曾经束缚着我。我常常在想，我该怎么办呢？后来我找到了一种很理想又特别有趣的状态，我希望我的绘画既能够呈现出中国传统的文化内涵，和中国的一些传统元素结合起来，同时也能够表现西方传统的，如巴洛克绘画思想的影响。对我来说，每一次的创作都是一次对话，一次与众不同、的两种文明之间的对话。”

伊瑞可以说是中国水墨艺术界的那条鲶鱼，闯出中国水墨艺术的一片全新的领域，同时也将中西这两种完全不同风格的绘画和谐地融为一体。伊瑞说，他还会在中国继续画下去，捷克“齐白石”的故事仍在中国继续书写着。

Scan for a Video

瑞典姑娘的中国梦

Swedish Girl's Dream in China

Swedish Girl's Dream in China

On the early morning of a midsummer day, a young couple walk hand in hand through a dense mountain forest, chatting and laughing. Their pace is slow as they sometimes stop to listen to birds chirping, or bend down to see the wildflowers on the roadside. The sunshine glimmers through the tree leaves, shining upon their youthful faces. The young man has black hair and brown eyes, typical for a Chinese young man, while the young woman has blonde hair and blue eyes. She is from Sweden, and her name is Miriam.

Miriam was born and brought up in Sweden. If not for the decision she made in 2015, she would not be here in this mountain forest of China, and nor would she be involved in this romance which transcends national borders.

In 2015, Miriam came to Fudan University in Shanghai to study as an exchange student. It was her first time to visit China. To her,

everything was new. The Chinese language was hard, but interesting. Shanghai was different from cities in her home country, and full of vitality. The lifestyles of the Shanghai people were also different from those of Swedish people, but also very colorful. Her life had begun a new chapter. She began learning Chinese and also Chinese culture, and embarked on a wonderful journey exploring Shanghai.

During her first semester, Miriam led an interesting and happy life. As a hardworking student, she had a full schedule every day. In the classroom, she was serious about each and every stroke when writing Chinese characters, and scrupulous when practicing pronunciation. She could often be seen in the lecture halls of Fudan University or in the library looking up interesting information.

Aside from being a hardworking student, Miriam is also an enthusiastic explorer. Besides wanting to learn more about China, she is also interested in the city of Shanghai and the lives of its people. She spends most of her leisure time in the city's streets and lanes. She loves to stroll around and feel the environment around her. She enjoys going to the Bund to enjoy the night scene amid the dazzling neon lights. She likes exploring unique, old buildings because their long histories reflect the vicissitudes of this oriental city. She also likes traveling to the Pudong New Area to see Shanghai's new look and feel the vitality of this modern metropolis.

But what she likes most is spending time in the city's small alleys where she can watch the hustle and bustle of people along the road, walk while eating a street snack, stop to listen to the happy laughter

of children, or look at handicrafts in the roadside stores. Not only did she see dazzling neon lights and towering buildings during her first six months in Shanghai, but also how ordinary people lived here in this thriving and unique city.

Half a year later, Miriam's first semester as an exchange student was drawing to an end. In her mind, Shanghai was no longer an abstract mark on the map, but rather a place where something amazing was happening everywhere, a place that always gave her surprises, a place that deserved savoring, and a place that had given her precious memories. As she saw, heard, and experienced more, it became clear to her that she had only seen a tiny portion of this huge country, and that there were still many more places to see and explore. Miriam wanted to gain a deeper understanding of China, its culture, and its language. Therefore, she chose to stay and continue her journey of exploring China.

Miriam began taking the train to visit more faraway places. She loves to travel by train because it not only allows her to enjoy the scenery on both sides of the railway, but also provides her opportunities to meet different types of people. She never feels lonely during these trips. She often chats with passengers and listens to their stories about local customs and practices, as they share their travel experiences.

Miriam's travels have taken her to bustling cities and tranquil rural towns where she has not only seen wonderful scenery and tasted delicious food, but she's also met with people who cherish life so much. She says that every person she has met, each food she has tried, and each place she has visited all help her learn more about China.

It was during these trips that Miriam realized what attracted her most were not the big metropolises, but rather those seemingly nondescript places in the countryside: a verdant hill, a tranquil mountain forest, a stream in the woods, a cluster of wild flowers, a small village at the foot of a hill, a small yard with drying grain, a simple rustic wall, and those unsophisticated but kind, smiling faces. In the mountains, there are beautiful scenes of which she never tires. There are countless natural treasures that always surprise her, myriads of beautiful folk handicrafts that dazzle her, and — above all — the many people whom she is fascinated by.

She's seen trees growing freely in the mountain forest, wild flowers blooming, butterflies dancing among flowering shrubs, and small insects crawling on grass leaves. She's seen people working in the fields, walking and enjoying the shade of the woods, and cooking simple but delicious daily meals with fresh ingredients like fresh mushrooms picked from the forest, a handful of green vegetables grown in the yard, a chunk of homemade tofu, and a few organic eggs. These are the traditional ways people cook in the countryside, with natural and healthy ingredients. Miriam has tried countless rural delicacies, like a plate of stir-fried green vegetables, or fried eggs in an iron wok, or a plate of cold tofu with sauce, or a bowl of fresh mushroom soup. In her eyes, life in the countryside is quiet and comfortable. It is a kind of life which is close to nature, a kind of life she desires most.

It was during her explorations around China that she found her greatest treasure: love. She met a young Chinese man with similar views about life, and they were drawn together. Despite their language and cultural differences, they got married in China in a traditional Chinese wedding. Miriam wore a traditional Chinese red wedding dress and stood side by side with her new husband. She says, "When I married him, I also married China."

Miriam is now a happy mother. She and her husband have a baby

who is a little bit of her and a little bit of him. Being both Chinese and Swedish, the child is the apple of their eye. Miriam says China has changed her and also changed the course of her life, and she will continue to embrace those changes in the days to come.

Miriam's hope is that she can live the life of which she has always dreamed. She looks forward to visiting more interesting and beautiful places, tasting more different kinds of Chinese food, and experiencing more Chinese culture. Whether it is in the south or the north, big cities or small villages, or traditional or modern, she is ready to visit, listen, and taste. It is also her hope that her family of three can settle down in a tranquil, countryside home that is close to nature so that they can enjoy nature's gifts with a grateful heart. She hopes to find a place where they can walk in the mountain forests and listen to chirping birds and gurgling springs. When they feel tired, they can sit leisurely on the hillside to watch the flowers and changing clouds. When they feel thirsty they can drink the spring water. When they feel hungry they can pick some wild fruit to eat. She says her home doesn't have to be large, but it should be quiet and cozy with sunshine streaming in through the window with beautiful clouds in the sky, and where each season presents a different scene. She says nature will be the most wonderful decorative painting in their home, and the sound of the wind and birds chirping will be their music. Their house will be surrounded by seasonal vegetables and fruit which they have planted themselves. Their meals will be simple, but teeming with natural flavor. Such a pace of life might seem slow in the eyes of others, but it is the kind of life that this family enjoys, and it is their source of happiness. To them, each moment is worth cherishing, and every detail worth savoring.

For Miriam, her dream is to explore the happiness and beauty of life with optimism and curiosity. It is a new dream for her, a dream that was born in China.

瑞典姑娘的中国梦

盛夏，清晨，一片茂密的山林间，一男一女手牵手走着，一边走一边轻声谈笑。他们走得很慢，有时停下来听听林间的鸟鸣，有时则俯下身去看看路边的野花。阳光透过树叶的缝隙洒下来，映亮了两人青春洋溢的笑脸：男的黑头发、黑眼睛，一看就是个地道的中国小伙子；而女的则是金发碧眼，一眼就能看出是个外国人。这个姑娘来自瑞典，叫 Miriam。

Miriam 是个地道的瑞典姑娘，在瑞典出生，在瑞典长大。如果没有 2015 年的那个决定，她的身影绝对不会出现在中国这片山林中，更不会有这段远隔千山万水的跨国情缘。

2015 年，还是大学生的 Miriam 决定以交换生的身份来中国留学。那是她第一次来到中国，第一次来到上海，也是第一次走进复旦大学的校门。对她来说，上海的一切都是新鲜的：汉语很难，可也很有意思；上海跟瑞典城市不一样，却处处充满生机；上海人的生活方式与瑞典人不同，可同样丰富多彩。生活从此打开全新的一页，她开始学习汉语，开始接触中国文化，开始自己神奇的上海探索之旅。

这一个学期中，她生活得充实而快乐。她首先是个勤奋的学生，每天的时间表都安排得满满的。在教室，她一笔一画地练习汉字，一丝不苟地练习发音；在图书馆，她一次次专注而投入地查阅自己感兴趣的资料；而复旦大学演讲厅里更是能时时见到她的身影。

在努力学习之外，Miriam还是一位兴致勃勃的探险家，她想了解中国，了解上海，了解上海人的生活。平日里，大部分课余时间她都是在上海的大街小巷中度过的。她兴致勃勃地四处闲逛，努力感受着身边的一切。去外滩看夜景，看满眼闪烁的霓虹；去看那些有着百年历史的特色老建筑，感受这座东方城市的岁月沧桑；去浦东新区看城市新貌，感受这座现代化大都市的勃勃生机。

她说，自己更喜欢的是在上海小巷中度过的那些时光：或是在路边看身边来来往往的行人；或是手举一份街头美味边走边吃；或是停下脚步听听孩子们的嬉笑声；或是在街边小店中面对一两件别致的手工艺品爱不释手。初来上海的半年中，她看到了这里的霓虹闪烁，看到了这里的高楼林立，更看到了属于这座城市特有的市井繁华，感受到了这里浓浓的人间烟火气。

半年后，一个学期的交换生生活眼看就要结束了。此时，在Miriam心中，上海已不再是地图上一个抽象的符号，而是一个处处充满神奇的地方，一个总是带给她无数惊喜的地方，一个值得她耐心品味的地方，一个带给她无数珍贵记忆的地方。在这里，她看的越多，听的越多，接触的越多，就越来越清楚地意识到，自己见到的只是中国这个国家的冰山一角，因为中国实在太大了，值得去的地方太多了，值得看的风景也太

多了。她想更深入地了解这个国家，了解它的文化和语言，于是她选

择留下来，继续自己的中国探索之旅。

此后，Miriam 开始坐着火车去更多更远的地方。她喜欢坐火车，因为坐火车不只可以欣赏铁路两边沿途的风光，更可以在火车上见到形形色色的人。火车上的时光，她从不觉得寂寞。她会跟身旁的人聊天，听他们讲中国各地的风土人情，也常常跟他们一起分享自己的旅行感受。

她去过很多繁华的城市，也去过不少宁静的山野村镇，看到了更美的风景，吃到了更多的美食，也遇到了更多热爱生活的人。她说，遇到的每个人，尝过的每种美食，见过的每处美景，都让她对中国的了解更多了一点。

也正是在这一次次旅行中，Miriam 逐渐意识到，真正吸引自己的，不是大城市，而是那些普通的中国乡村，是那些特别不起眼的地方。一座苍翠的小山，一片寂静的山林，林间的一道小溪，溪边的一丛野花，山下一个小小的村庄，一座晒满谷物的小院，一道质朴的篱笆墙，墙内几张质朴和善的笑脸，都是她眼中最美的风景。在大山里，有她永远看不厌的美景，有数不清的带给她惊喜的大自然中的宝贝，有让她眼花缭乱的民间手工艺品，更有许多让她着迷并愿意亲近的人。

她看见，山林间树木在自由生长，野花在自由绽放，蝴蝶在花丛中自在飞舞，小虫在草叶上缓缓爬行。她看见，人们在田间劳作，在林间散步乘凉，用最新鲜的食材、最传统的方式烹制简单而可口的一日三餐。几朵山林间采摘的蘑菇，一把自家院子里种植的青菜，一大块自制的豆腐，几颗名副其实的柴鸡蛋，都是最天然最健康的食材。她吃过数不清的乡野美味，有时是一盘绿油油的素炒青菜，有时是一盘简单的铁锅炒鸡蛋，有时是一盘凉拌豆腐，有时则是一碗鲜味十足的菌菇汤。在她眼中，乡村的生活宁静而美好，是最贴近大自然的生活，也是她最向往的生活。

在这一次次探索中国的旅行中，她还有了一个更大的收获——遇到了爱情。她和他，一个瑞典人，一个中国人，因为相近的生活态度而彼此吸引，并认定对方是自己愿意共享幸福的那个人。他们最终跨越语言和文化的巨大差异走到了一起。她和他，在中国举行了一场传统的中国式婚礼。那天，她穿上一件大红的中国传统嫁衣，与最心爱的他站在了一起。她说，我嫁给了他，也嫁给了中国。

现在的Miriam已经是一个幸福的妈妈。她和丈夫有了一个宝宝，这个孩子一半儿像她，一半儿像他，身体里流淌着中国和瑞典的血液，是父母最珍视的宝贝。Miriam说，中国改变了她的生活轨迹，也改变了她，而她会继续为中国改变下去。

她希望今后的每一天都能以自己梦想的方式生活。她希望去更多有意思的地方，去看更多的中国美景，去尝更多的中国美食，去感受更多的中国风情。无论是南方还是北方，无论是大城市还是小村庄；无论是传统的还是现代的，她都希望去看看，去听听，去尝尝。她还希望一家三口在山野间找一处宁静的居所，与大自然比邻而居，带着一颗感恩的心享受大自然的馈赠：闲暇时带孩子

在山林间漫步，倾听鸟儿的歌唱，聆听泉水的欢歌；累时与家人在山坡上闲坐，静观花开花落，云卷云舒；渴了掬一捧山泉入口，饿了摘几颗山果充饥。她的家不用很大，但一定宁静而温馨：窗外阳光和煦，天高云淡，四时风景不同，大自然是家中最美的装饰画，风声、鸟鸣是家中最动听的音乐；房前屋后，满眼都是自家种植的四时蔬果，一日三餐简单却充满浓浓的自然风味。或许在别人看来，这样的生活节奏很慢，但是他们享受的就是这样一种慢生活，因为这样的生活里有他们心中全部的幸福与美好，每一个瞬间都值得珍惜，每一处细节都值得品味。

对Miriam来说，带着一份乐观，带着一颗好奇的心，不断去探索生活的幸福与美好，是她的梦想，一个全新的梦想，这个梦想始于中国。

Scan for a Video
坊间印象
FOLK HANDICRAFTS

外国记者眼中的中国共享经济

China's Sharing Economy

China's Sharing Economy

It is six o'clock in the morning in Beijing's Chaoyang District, and Christ, is leaving for work. It will take him more than ten minutes to walk to the subway station, about one kilometer away. To save time, he opens an App on his mobile phone, scans the QR code on a shared bike and unlocks it. He rides the bike to the station which helps him catch the first train. After arriving at work, Christ collects the documents he needs, leaves, and hails a car with another App on his phone. He is going to see a client today, and the ride will save time over a crowded bus during morning rush hour. After concluding his meeting with the client, it begins raining. Since he didn't bring an umbrella, he decides to rent one, also with an App. Such shared umbrellas don't need to be returned to their original pick-up point because there are many return places available. Opening his umbrella, Christ walks along the bustling street.

The Australian man came to China in 2000 to study. After graduation, he chose to stay in Beijing and work for a financial news outlet. He has not only witnessed China's booming "sharing economy", but also benefits from it. Besides sharing bikes, cars and umbrellas, one can also share big things like apartments and houses or small items like basketballs and portable power chargers, which are all the rage across China and have become an indispensable part of daily life.

Statistics conducted by the news outlet Christ works for show that in 2016 a total of 600 million people participated in such sharing economy activities in China with a trade volume amounting to 500 billion US dollars. By 2020, the sharing economy will make up 10% of the country's GDP. What's the driving force behind such huge numbers? As early as 1978, the term "sharing economy" was proposed by American sociology professors Marcus Felson and Joel Spaeth. Today, using such digital tools like GPS, software and smart phones allows the mobile use of idle resources, resulting in much more convenience in daily life. According to a survey, Chinese mobile payments tripled in 2016 compared to the previous year, reaching 5.5 trillion US dollars, whereas the American market has increased by 39%. China is now the world's largest mobile payment market. Why is China leading this trend? What are the characteristics of the Chinese sharing economy? How does it differ from the American or European sharing economies?

As a business reporter, Christ once interviewed Professor Jeffery Towson from Peking University, who is an expert in investment. In Professor Towson's view, China's advantage in developing the sharing economy lies mainly in its huge population of consumers. The number of smart phone and mobile payment users in China is much larger than anywhere else in the world. Despite this, the sharing economy in China is also faced with growing challenges and problems. For example, traffic congestion in many Chinese cities can negatively influence car hailing services. This is more pronounced in Beijing than in New York. For China, this presents an opportunity and also a challenge. In order for its sharing economy to flourish, the country has more tough nuts to crack.

Regarding Beijing's serious traffic jams, Professor Rong Ke from Tsinghua University echoes the opinion of Jeffery Towson. Professor Rong was also interviewed by Christ, and he believes more services are needed to solve this problem. Software Apps like online car hailing and bike-sharing were created to ease traffic jams, which have significantly reduced the cost of transportation. The gist of the sharing economy lies not only in sharing, but also in efficiency. In other words, reducing costs is the core value of the sharing economy.

Economists focus on ways to improve economic efficiency, while consumers focus on convenience such as sharing items, mobile payments and pay-per-use services which have never been experienced before. That said, is such an "access economy" featuring high efficiency the same as the traditional "rental" economy?

According to Professor Rong Ke, the current Chinese sharing economy is quite different from the traditional rental economy. The latter refers to a situation in which the person's budget is too limited to afford an item and thus rents it, while the former lays more emphasis on how to get the service. To the company which provides access to service, both new and idle resources can be used. Uber (user-to-user) and bike-sharing (platform-to-user) are both part of the sharing economy. Some may argue that bike-sharing is a type of rental service, while Uber is more of a sharing service. The fact is that Uber has long been in cooperation with some small car rental firms to meet the huge customer demand through its platform. It would be an impossible mission if Uber only relied on sharing cars among its customers.

Car and bicycle rental companies are not something new, and have been around for quite a long time. How is it that they have become an inseparable part of the sharing economy that is now all the rage? Professor Towson asserts that the digital revolution is the fundamental reason behind the trend, which features the combination of various kinds of software with smart phones, GPS and mobile payments. The development of such new technologies has brought about drastic changes to the access economy. Renting a bike is nothing new, but what impresses people is the advent of the software which makes the process so convenient. Take Uber, for example. Whether using cars purchased by Uber, by partnering with a car rental firm, or by registered drivers — these are all different forms of service of the same nature. The key is that they capitalize on unprecedented technology which greatly improves the convenience of these ready-to-use services. Therefore, the sharing economy can be seen as the digitalization of such services.

Indeed, frontrunner companies like Didi, Meituan and Uber have played an important role in the growth of the sharing economy. In addition, many investment firms have also made significant contributions. For example, the apartment sharing company Tujia acquired an investment of 300 million US dollars in 2016. Many bike-sharing companies have also gained several hundred million dollars in investment. Why are these investment firms willing to put in so much money? Can they make a profit?

Professor Rong Ke believes there should be no need to worry about this because clever venture capital investors already understand the business model of the sharing economy. Having carefully studied the model of bike-sharing companies, Rong found at least two ways such businesses profit. To begin with, each bike is used four to six times per day at over 1,000 times in one year, which is more than enough to cover the bike's cost. More importantly, the bikes can record relevant data of the rider's last kilometer, which has significant value.

It is important to note, however, that excess investment may create the risk of an economic bubble. According to Professor Towson, there are different types of bubbles, among which the credit bubble is one of the most common. But the situation in China is a little different from that of other countries. Take the US as an example, where a new enterprise may receive investments from various sources of venture capital. Among the many investing companies in China, however, Alibaba, Baidu and Tencent are the three major players. Their investment models are different from those of other venture capital investors where instead of focusing on profits, they focus on other aspects.

These three large companies dominate the investment and formation of the Chinese ecosystem, but their interests are different. Rather than focusing on making or losing money, which is quite normal for venture capital investors, these Internet companies often place more emphases on gaining a market share, obtaining data, and establishing their own systems and enterprises.

Professor Rong Ke and the founder of a bike-sharing brand calculated that based on the current usage, the industry can make an annual profit of one billion yuan or more. The professor also stresses that these bike-sharing companies should not be only viewed as service providers, but also as financial enterprises. They have turned their services into financial assets as they receive a steady cash flow every day. As a result, venture capital investors will consider them good investments, and will be willing to put in more money.

The government will also play a key role in the sustainable growth of the sharing economy in China. Besides supervising how companies provide services, the government should also keep watch on user behavior. With the digitalization in various fields such as transportation, retailing, finance and insurance, the sharing economy and access services can be promoted in areas with low efficiency but high demand provided that the usage cost is greatly reduced, thus creating a bright future for China's sharing economy.

外国记者眼中的中国共享经济

早上六点，住在北京市朝阳区的Christ走出家门，打算坐地铁去公司。他家离地铁站不到一公里，可是走过去也要十多分钟。Christ赶时间，他在小区门口点开手机APP，扫码解锁了一辆共享单车，骑车到地铁站，刚好赶上了头班地铁。到公司之后，他整理好需要的文件，用手机约了一辆网约车。今天他要去拜访客户，早高峰的公交车上，人实在太多了，能够搭上私家车主的顺风车，真是太方便了。从客户公司出来，天下起了雨。他没带伞，就在楼下租

了一把共享雨伞，这种雨伞借用完以后，可以在很多地方还，不用特意还到原来的借用点。Christ撑起伞走上街道，汇入来来往往的人流当中。来自澳大利亚的Christ，2000年到中国留学，毕业后留在北京，在财经媒体工作。他亲眼见证并参与了共享经济在中国的发展，不只是自行车、汽车、雨伞，大到公寓住房，小到篮球、充电宝，共享经济正在中国掀起浪潮，成为人们日常生活中不可缺少的一部分。

Christ所任职的财经媒体曾做过相关统计：2016年，中国共计6亿人参与到共享经济相关活动中，交易额达5000亿美元。到2020年，共享经济将占中国GDP总量

的10%。这巨大的数据背后的真正动力是什么？早在1978年，“共享经济”这个术语就已经被美国的两位社会学教授马科斯·费尔逊（Marcus Felson）和琼·斯潘思（Joel Spaeth）提出。今天，从GPS到软件再到智能手机，数字化的工具让闲置的资源流动起来，人们的生活在共享中变得越来越便捷。据调查，2016年中国移动支付市场增加了两倍，达5.5万亿美元，相比较美国移动支付增长了39%，中国已经形成了全球最大的移动支付市场。为什么引领这场变革的会是中国？中国共享经济的特点是什么？它和美国或者欧洲的共享经济比起来有何不同？

作为专职财经记者的Christ曾采访过北京大学研究投资领域的Jeffery Towson教授。Towson教授认为，中国发展共享经济的优势首先在于消费者数量巨大。中国使用智能手机的人口、使用移动支付的人口比世界上其他地方都多得多。但同时中国的共享经济也面临着更大的挑战和更多的问题。比如，在提供服务方面，中国城市的交通堵塞很严重，北京比纽约更拥堵，这既是机会，也是挑战，中国在发展共享经济方面其实需要解决更多严峻的问题。

就北京交通堵塞严重这一问题，另一位受访者清华大学的戎珂教授也很认同Towson教授的观点。他认为，正因如此，才需要更多服务解决这个问题，像网约车和共享单车这类共享交通软件的诞生就是为了解决拥堵问题，共享汽车、共享自行车大大降低了即用成本。共享经济不在于分享，而在于效率。降低即用成本是共享经济的核心所在。

当然，经济学家看到的是提高经济效率，但是从消费者的角度来看，他们看到的不是效率，而是方便。他们体验到的是前所未有的方便——共享物品，移动支付，即付即用。那么这种高效率的即用型经济是否就是传统意义上的租赁经济呢？

戎珂教授认为，时下中国的共享经济和传统的租赁经济还是有很大的差别的。租赁经济指的是预算有限、没有足够的钱购买一样东西，因此去租来用；但是共享经济注重的是如何获得服务，就提供服务使用权的公司来说，无论新资源还是闲置资源都是一样的。无论是主打用户对用户分享的优步还是主打平台对用户的共享单车，都是共享经济。也许有人认为共享单车是租，优步是共享，但是事实上，优步很早就已经和一些小

型轿车租赁公司合作，通过优步平台来满足巨大的用户需求。如果只依赖于共享用户自己的闲置车辆资源，优步是无法为平台大量的用户提供足够的服务的。

汽车、自行车租赁公司并不是什么新鲜事物，很早就一直存在，为什么突然就能搭上共享经济的浪潮，成为新风尚呢？Towson 教授认为，使现在中国的共享经济成为浪潮的根本原因是数字化变革，各种软件结合智能手机、GPS、移动支付……新技术的发展急剧转变着即用型经济。租自行车不新鲜，新的是出现了这种软件，可以让租自行车变得无比方便。就拿优步来说，无论是自己买车还是与租车公司合作，还是使用用户自己的车，本质上都没有改变，关键的是他们利用前所未有的技术工具把这种即用型服务的便利性大大提高了，因此，共享经济是对即用型服务的数字化。

在共享经济的发展过程中，滴滴、美团、优步这些走在前列的运营公司当然发挥了重要作用。另一方面，大力推动中国共享经济的是很多投资公司。比如途家，一家做公寓租赁共享的公司，2016年获得了3亿美元的投资，各个共享单车品牌也从投资者手中获得数亿美元。这些投资公司为什么愿意为这类公司投这么多钱？投资公司能赢利吗？

对此，戎珂教授认为无需过虑，因为风险投资商都很聪明。他们明白了共享经济的业务模式就会投资。戎珂教授深入研究了共享单车的业务模式，发现他们可以从至少两个方面获得收益。首先是每天的运营，每天每辆单车大约被使用四到六次，一年下来就超过一千次，轻而易举就能收回一辆单车的成本。第二，也是最重要的，是数据的价值。共享单车会记录用户最后一公里的行为数据，这些数据很有价值，是生态系统价值。

当然，过度的投资有可能产生出现泡沫的危险。Towson教授认为，泡沫有不同种类，大部分人说到泡沫指的是信贷泡沫。但有一点中国和别国不同，在美国，为创业公司投资的有各种不同的创投资本，而看中国的饼图，虽然也有很多创业投资商，但是有三家公司提供了绝大部分的资金——阿里巴巴、百度和腾讯。他们投资的方式和一般的创投不同，他们关注的重点不是利润，而是其他的方面。这也是中国独特的地方，就是在投资建设该生态系统上，是三家公司占据主导地位，他们关切的利益各不相同。这当中必定有人会赚钱，有人会亏钱，但是创投商本就如此。互联网公司初期关注的不是利润，而是市场份额，获取数据，建设自己的系统和企业。

戎珂教授和某共享单车品牌的创立者测算过他们的利润问题，以目前的使用量来看，除去生产及维护成本，一年的利润是10亿元，甚至更多。他同时强调，这些共享单车公司其实不仅仅是服务公司，也是金融公司，因为他们把服务金融化了，每天都能看到稳定的现金流流入，所以创投才会觉得他们是良好的金融资产，才会给予更多的投资。

当然，面对未来，共享经济要持续长期发展，除了消费者和公司以外，政府也扮演着关键的角色。政府既要监管公司如何提供服务，还要监管用户行为。

随着各个领域的数字化变革，交通、零售、金融保险等行业，只要能大大降低使用成本，在本来效率不高、需求却很高的领域都可以推行共享经济、即用服务。中国的共享经济必将迎来更加长足的发展。

Scan for a Video

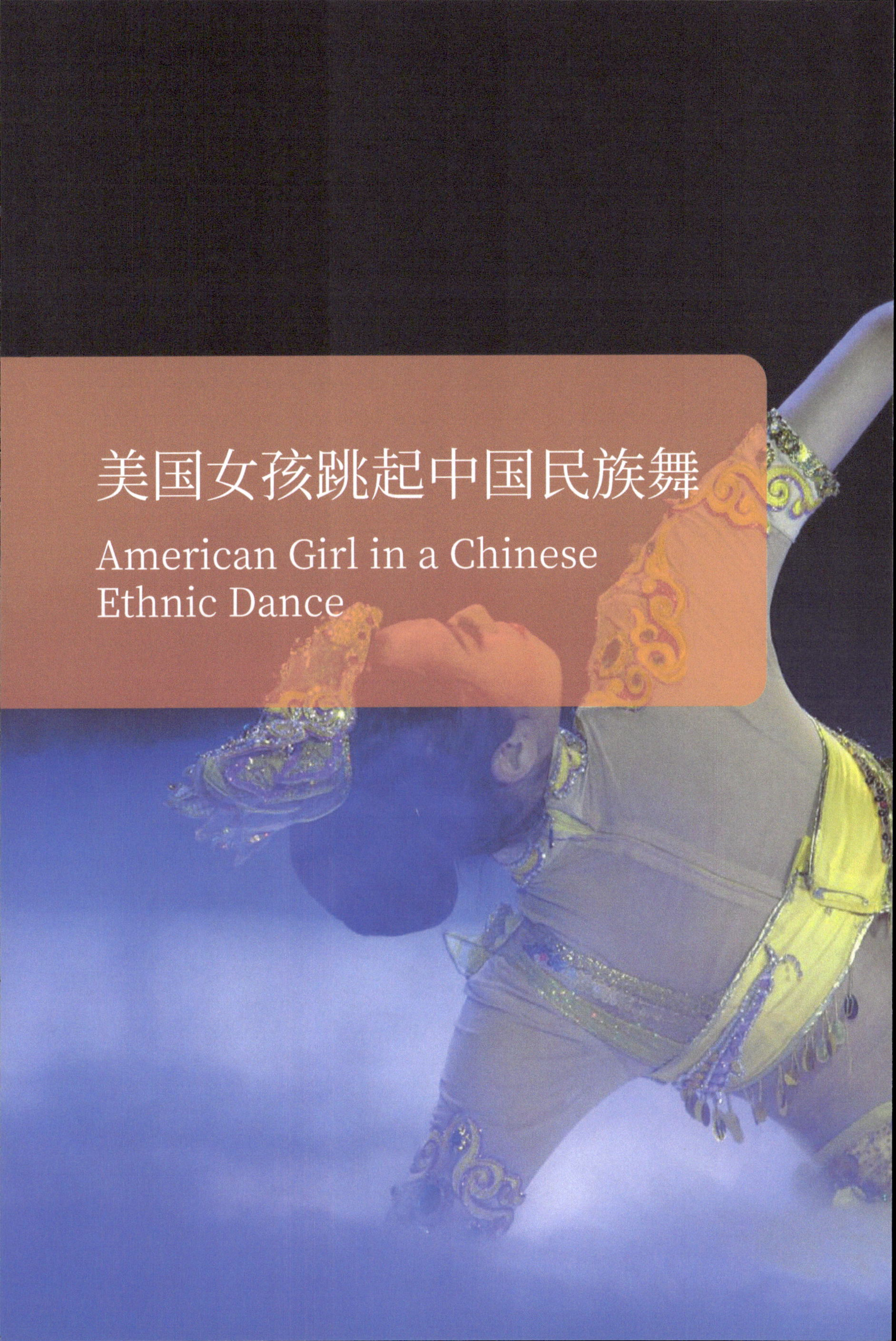
美国女孩跳起中国民族舞
American Girl in a Chinese Ethnic Dance

American Girl in a Chinese Ethnic Dance

It is early morning at the Minzu University of China in Beijing's Haidian District, the campus is still wet with dew as if it'd just awoken. An eye-catching red figure has already shown up at the gate of the Dance College. She goes into the dance studio, changes into a black leotard, and begins flexing her leg muscles and stretching her waist. Her movements are soft, but powerful. This girl, brimming with happiness and joy, is a student of the Dance College of the university. Her name is Ellie.

Ellie is from San Francisco, US. She always wears her brown hair in a bun, displaying her smooth forehead. When she speaks, her big eyes are like crescent moons, and when she laughs it reveals her beautiful teeth. She is an American girl: optimistic, confident, and free of constraint. But few had expected that she would become so infatuated

with Chinese ethnic dance and find her dream in the East through dancing. In 2015, Ellie left her hometown and traveled all the way to Beijing to become a student at the Dance College of the Minzu University of China. Since then, Chinese ethnic dance has become part of her life.

Speaking of her close bond with Chinese ethnic dance, Ellie is excited as she recalls the scene several years ago when she watched a dance performance in the US entitled "Spirit of the Peacock" by renowned Chinese dancer Yang Liping. The dance demonstrated not only the outer beauty of the peacock, but also an internal passion for life. Through a series of agile moves, the dancer's flexible body brought the bird to life. At that moment, Ellie felt a pulsing deep within her, as if a peacock were calling to her, and she was overwhelmed with the performance. It was at that moment she'd made up her mind to learn this dance which was totally unfamiliar to her. At first, she tried to learn the dance in a dancing class with Chinese children and older women in the US. "Our study was quite amateurish, but I felt very happy dancing with them, " she says. It was the joy Ellie felt during this process of watching and practicing Chinese ethnic dancing that led to her decision to travel across the ocean to China to study the art professionally.

In the eyes of some people, studying dance may seem a bit boring because students usually spend most of their time practicing basic skills and repeating moves that have already been learned. But Ellie never gets tired of it, and she takes great pleasure in practicing the moves. To her, studying Chinese ethnic dance has allowed her to re-understand her own body, and to discover more possibilities to incorporate strength and beauty. Ellie has been studying ballet since childhood. In ballet, the hand position rarely changes while there are many leg movements. This has been her deepest impression of dance. It was not until she started learning Chinese ethnic dance that she realized the huge difference between these two types of dance, such as the various hand postures in Chinese dance. In the Dai dance style, for example, the hands form different shapes which imitate the movements of the peacock's claws and beak. These are called the "palm-shaped," "claw-shaped," and "beak-shaped" hands. In the Uygur style, there are the "hat-holding", "wrist-circling" and "finger-snapping" hands, which are all done in coordination with the action of the performer's head so as to present the audience an expression filled with passion. "These hand postures are so amazing! When performing these dances, I feel my body has been awakened, " Ellie says delightedly while demonstrating the hand postures and blinking her grayish blue eyes.

It was during this process of studying Chinese ethnic dance that Ellie really began to grasp the concept of China being a "multi-ethnic country," which she had read about before. "After learning the dance of one Chinese ethnic group, I felt I had gained a deeper understanding of that group's cultural heritage and the people." She then shows the Mongolian dance based on her understanding. Striding and shaking her shoulders, she dances wildly and passionately as she stretches and contracts her limbs, looking just like a Mongolian girl roaming the grassland with horses, cattle, and sheep beneath the blue sky and white clouds. After finishing the dance, she says, "The Mongolians live on the vast grassland, which has a direct influence on their dancing style.

When performing this dance, I feel free and unrestrained because the grassland is free and boundless." She says that every time she performs the Mongolian dance, she feels likes she is really riding a galloping horse across the northern grasslands. The Peacock Dance of the Dai ethnic group, the Sainaimu Dance of the Uygur ethnic group (which stresses the expression of warm feelings), and the passionate Andai Dance of the Mongolian ethnic group all make her use her body differently. This physicality associated with the dances has enlightened her understanding of the wide cultural diversity of these ethnic groups throughout the vast territory of China. Through these dances, she also feels the emotional bloodlines the people have with their dances, with their culture, and with the land itself. Through the process of learning Chinese ethnic dance, this beautiful American girl has come to truly understand this colorful nation with its 56 ethnic groups, and has fallen in love with this wonderful, harmonious, and dynamic country.

Because of her love and understanding of Chinese dance, Ellie set up the website "World of Chinese Dance" which introduces Chinese ethnic dances to viewers and also offers teaching tutorials. She did this because there was a lack of relevant information available when she was trying to learn these dances before she came to China, so she hopes the website can help those who are interested in the art. Though she is still busy learning the dances, Ellie will often post her experiences, upload videos and tutorials, and do her best to maintain the website. In her opinion, learning Chinese ethnic dance is not only about dancing with your heart and feeling the dance, but also about understanding its beauty and charm. She feels a great national culture of a country should be the treasure of the whole world. A bit shyly, Ellie says with pride, "I want to introduce Chinese ethnic dance to friends across the globe, and give them a chance to learn more about this art form. My dream is to become a great dancer in this field." Ellie is attracted to the vitality and great diversity of Chinese ethnic dance, which has inspired her to want to share it with the world. More people like Ellie are needed for the global civilization to continue to develop and prosper, for only in this way can our world be blessed with harmony and cultural diversity.

美国女孩跳起中国民族舞

清晨，位于北京海淀区中关村南大街27号的中央民族大学校园还带着夜里的露气，似乎刚从睡梦中醒来，一个亮眼的红色身影就出现在舞蹈学院的门前。她打开舞蹈室的门，换上一袭黑色的练功服后就开始压腿，舒展腰肢，动作柔软而有力，一气呵成。这个从四肢到脸庞都洋溢着愉悦的女孩是中央民族大学舞蹈学院的学生——艾丽。

艾丽来自美国旧金山，她那褚色的头发总是扎成一个髻，露出光洁的额头，一说话的时候大大的眼睛就像月亮弯弯。她很爱笑，笑的时候毫不吝惜地咧开嘴巴露出整齐

的牙齿，是典型的乐观、自信、不羁的美国女孩模样。谁曾想到，这个美国女孩痴迷于中国的民族舞蹈，用身体的舞动在遥远的东方寻找到了自己的梦想。2015 年，艾丽离开自己的家乡漂洋过海来到中国北京，成为中央民族大学舞蹈学院的一名学生。从此，她与中国民族舞结下了不解之缘。

说起和中国民族舞结缘的故事，艾丽带着兴奋又向往的表情回忆起自己几年前在美国看到的杨丽萍的舞蹈表演——《雀之灵》。杨丽萍的舞蹈表现出孔雀外在的美丽和内在的生命激情，她柔软的身体在灵活的动作下演绎出孔雀的灵动。那一刻，艾丽感受到血管深处一种生命的跳动，仿佛有一只孔雀在呼唤自己。她被杨丽萍演绎的中国民族舞感动了。于是，她决定要学习当时对她来说还很陌生的舞蹈。可是在当时的艾丽看来，中国是那么遥远又陌生的国度，民

族舞到底怎么跳也是一件未知的事。在决定来中国学习民族舞蹈之前，艾丽经历几番周折在美国跟着小朋友、阿姨们一起学习中国舞蹈。“虽然我们的学习很业余，但是和她们一起跳我感到很快乐。”正是欣赏、练习中国民族舞过程中的快乐让艾丽下定决心远渡重洋，去中国专业学习中国民族舞。

在旁人看来，在中央民族大学舞蹈学院的学习有点儿枯燥，每天大部分时间都是练习基本功、重复学习过的舞蹈动作，但艾丽却乐此不疲，反复练习舞蹈时总是心情愉悦。在艾丽看来，学习中国民族舞蹈让她重新认识了自己的身体，探索、发现了自己身体力量与柔美的更多可能性。艾丽从幼时就开始学习芭蕾舞，芭蕾舞的手位比较固定、腿部动作特别丰富，这是舞蹈刻在艾丽记忆中最深的印象。学习了中国民族舞蹈后，艾丽意识到中国的民族舞蹈和芭蕾舞差别很大，舞蹈的姿态也千差万变：傣族舞的掌型手、爪形手、嘴型手分别模仿孔雀身体的活动、孔雀的爪子和孔雀的嘴巴，将孔雀的模样演绎得淋漓尽致；维吾尔族舞蹈的托帽手、绕腕手、弹指手尽量用手的动作配合头部的活动，将热情的表情传递给观舞者。“这些手的动作真是太迷人了！跳着中国的民族舞蹈，我感觉自己的身体被舞蹈重新唤醒了。”艾丽一边示范民族舞的手部动作，一边眨着蓝灰色的眼睛愉快地说着。

在学习中国民族舞蹈的过程中，艾丽觉得自己才真正了解了以前通过阅读学到的中国是个多民族国家的含义。“我学到中国一个民族的舞蹈，就会从舞蹈中感受到这个民族的文化底蕴，就认识了中国的一个民族。”艾丽开始为大家展示她所理解的蒙古族的舞蹈。在阔步抖肩的表演中，艾丽随着肢体的开合呈现出自由、奔放的神态，仿佛是蒙古

族少女在辽阔的草原上伴着骏马牛羊、蓝天白云徜徉。跳完蒙古舞后，艾丽谈到："蒙古族住在辽阔的草原上，这直接影响到了他们的舞蹈。我跳蒙古舞的时候觉得特别自由、无拘束，整个动作是大方的而不是娇柔的，因为草原就是无垠的、自由的。"每次跳完蒙古舞，艾丽都觉得自己好似真的在风吹草低见牛羊的北方草原上策马奔驰。傣族舞中模仿孔雀的孔雀舞，维吾尔族舞中强调亲切情感表达的赛乃姆舞，蒙古舞中来自草原自由奔放的安代舞……这些多种多样的民族舞蹈都让艾丽用肢体动作深切感受到中国广阔土地上民族的多样性，也感受到民族舞蹈和民族文化、土地紧密相依的情感血脉。正是在跳中国民族舞的过程中，美国女孩艾丽理解了拥有56个民族、多姿多彩的中国，爱上了美丽和谐、充满生命力的中国。

因为热爱和理解，艾丽在中央民族大学学习中国民族舞的同时创建了一个介绍和教授中国民族舞的网站——World of Chinese Dance。她创立这个网站是因为她自己作为外国人学习中国民族舞之初缺少相关的信息和渠道去学习，所以她想要为更多对中国民族舞感兴趣的人提供一个窗口。于是，在忙碌、辛苦的舞蹈学习过程中，艾丽会把自己学习中国民族舞的体会、跳舞的视频和教程传到网站上，花一定时间进行网站的维护。在她看来，学习中国民族舞不仅仅是用心地跳好、感受每一支舞蹈，还需要把中国民族舞的美和魅力展现给更多的人欣赏。一个国家优秀的民族文化应该是全世界的瑰宝。艾丽带着羞涩又骄傲的表情说："我想把中国民族舞介绍给全世界的朋友们，让他们有机会多了解一点儿中国民族舞。我的梦想就是成为中国民族舞的舞蹈家！”中国的民族舞展示的生命力与多样性不仅吸引着艾丽，也唤起了艾丽传播中国民族舞的梦想。世界文化的发展与繁荣、人类文明的繁衍与昌盛，需要更多的像艾丽这样的人，才能实现“美美与共，天下大同”。

Scan for a Video

洛克在中国

Locke's Life in China

Locke's Life in China

In the rehearsal room of the National Academy of Chinese Theatre Arts, we met a special student. He was speaking authentic Chinese and learning the basic skills of Beijing Opera such as showing a single finger, blinking, and continuous stepping. Although his movements were a little bit awkward, he practiced hard and performed well. His name is Locke, and he is an international student from Canada.

Locke is a student of the Communication University of China, and he has been living in Beijing for five years. Because of his love for Chinese opera, particularly his interest in the characters, facial makeup, costumes, etc., he had come to China specifically to learn authentic Chinese opera. "I think Chinese opera has something in common with Western opera, but the former has many special features," Locke told us. "Chinese operas are more complicated because they require all types of hand, eye and body gestures and steps. When I see the actors or actresses perform on stage, I always feel that their performances are very easy and natural. But once I started to learn Chinese opera myself, I really began to understand the meaning

of the saying 'Performing one minute on the stage requires rehearsing ten years off the stage.' These performances are really not easy. It takes actors or actresses a lot of time to learn and master the skills required for even a simple performance."

Locke's daily life is very colorful. In addition to studying Chinese opera, he likes walking around and visiting scenic spots in Beijing, including the hutongs, Qianmen Street, Beihai Park, and the Drum Tower. "Having lived in Beijing for five years has really helped me acquire a new understanding of China. The mobile phone is an indispensible tool in China. Usually I go out only with a mobile phone, and I can do everything. I can swipe it when I take the bus, the subway or even ride a bike. I can also swipe it to go shopping, eat at a restaurant or watch a movie. When you don't want to go out, you can order takeout. When you need to buy something, you don't need to go out. You can buy everything you need online just by placing an order on your phone. My friends and I often feel as if we spend most of our time either picking up goods sent by express delivery or we're on the way to do so, ha ha!"

Locke often shares his experience of living in China with his foreign friends. "In the beginning, they thought I was bragging. Later, I invited them to visit China and see for themselves. They were astonished and envious of the modern way of life in China." Recalling his experience of returning to Canada during his vacation, Locke laughs again. "I'm used to living in China without cash when I go out. When I returned to Canada, I was not used to it. When I went out, I forgot to bring cash and I couldn't do anything. It was really inconvenient."

In addition to the convenience of mobile phone payments, Locke thinks that transportation in China is also quite convenient. "Because China is such a big country, it is very convenient and fast to travel from one place to another because of the high-speed rail network that extends in all directions. I like to take the high-speed trains to different cities to explore different parts of China."

When asked what he likes most in China, Locke replied "Chinese food" without hesitation. "There are so many delicious kinds of food in China. When I go shopping, if I see some delicious food I haven't eaten before, I want to taste it. But my favorite food is dumplings. I think dumplings are a particularly important food for Chinese people, and more often than not, they represent a kind of bond. Chinese people eat dumplings on Spring Festival or other festivals. In the process of making dumplings, the whole family will get together and happily participate, which is a wonderful experience. Though they are a homely food, dumplings have a deep meaning behind them." Locke recalled that he was invited to a friend's house to make dumplings. "In

the beginning, I didn't know how to make dumplings at all. I watched everyone else make them with ease, so I thought I only needed to pinch the edges of the wrappers together. Later I found that making dumplings required a lot of skill. It took me a long time to master this, but now I can make pretty good dumplings myself."

Recalling his colorful life in China for the five years, Locke believes that the most important prerequisite for helping him gain so

many unforgettable experiences was his willingness to speak and communicate with different people. "I love to wander the city and go to the hutongs to play with the children, teach them English, and chat with old men in the streets about everything under the sun. I think I speak Chinese very well because I'm willing to talk. I think no matter what country you come from, as long as you are willing to open your mouth, you can narrow the distance between each other through communication. Anyone who is willing to communicate will certainly benefit a lot."

One thing Locke is very proud of is that he has made many friends from all over China, and he has learned some dialects of different parts of China. He likes the dialect of northeast China best. Locke then gave us a northern dialect performance for us right then and there. “What are you doing? Come on, young man, who are you looking at? I am looking at you. Will you take another look at me? I will take another look at you.” There is also a Cantonese tongue twister which has become popular online recently, known as: “Each country has its own national anthem.” He can also master the different tones of Cantonese and speaks it quite well.

“I want to learn more about China. If I have the chance, I want to visit different cities and learn more about Chinese culture.” He also made the sign of a heart with his arms, saying “I love China! China, I love you!”

洛克在中国

在中国戏曲学院的练习室里，我们见到了一位特别的学生。他操着一口地道的中文，正跟着老师学习单指、转眼、连步等各种京剧基本动作，虽然动作略显生涩，但他一板一眼练得很认真，看起来还挺像那么回事。他就是来自加拿大的留学生洛克（Locke）。

洛克是中国传媒大学的学生，已经在北京生活五年了。因为喜爱中国戏曲，对中国戏曲中的各种行当、脸谱、戏服等特别感兴趣，所以他特地来中国学习地道的中国戏曲。“我觉得中国的戏曲有点儿像西方的歌剧，但是又有很多特别的地方。”洛克微笑着说，“中国的戏曲更加复杂，因为有各种

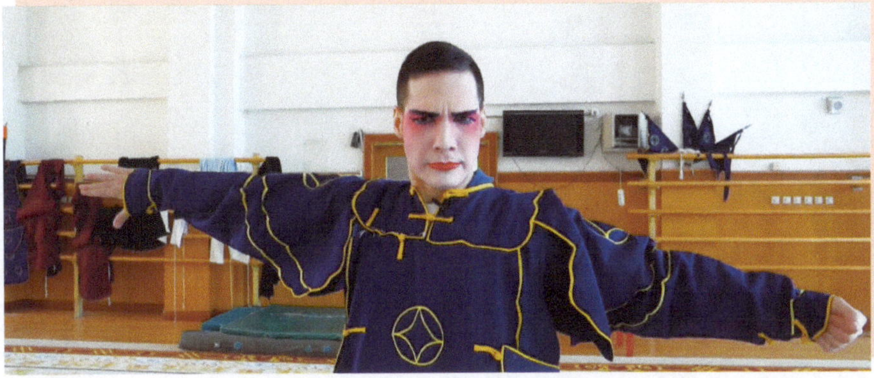

各样的手眼身法步。我在台下看台上的演员表演的时候，总觉得他们的表演看上去轻轻松松，展现得非常自然，但是当我自己开始学习中国戏曲之后，我才真正明白什么叫‘台上一分钟，台下十年功’，这些表演实在太不容易了。舞台上看起来简单的表演，实际上演员们需要花费很多很多时间才能学会和掌握。”

洛克的日常生活十分丰富，除了学习中国戏曲，他最爱在北京城里四处走走、看看。北京的各大胡同，前门大街、北海公园、鼓楼……到处都留下了洛克的身影。“在北京生活的这五年，真的完全刷新和颠覆了我对中国的认识。生活在中国，平日里最必不可少的物件就是手机。平时出门，只需要一部手机就可以解决所有的问题。出门坐公交、坐地铁甚至骑自行车都可以刷手机；去商

场购物、吃饭、看电影也都可以刷手机。”“当你不想出

门的时候，你可以点外卖。需要买东西的时候，基本不用出门，只需要在手机上下单就可以在网上买到所有你需要的东西。”洛克大笑着说，“我和朋友常常感叹，我们平时大部分时间不是在取快递，就是在取快递的路上。哈哈哈！”

洛克时常和自己的外国朋友分享自己在中国生活的经历。“一开始他们都觉得我在吹牛，后来我邀请他们亲自来中国看看，大家都震惊了，都特别羡慕中国这种新型的生活方式。”回忆起自己假期回加拿大的经历，洛克又笑了，“习惯了在中国出门不需要带现金的生活，回到加拿大我真的好不习惯。有几次忘记带现金出门，结果什么事情都办不成，真的太不方便了。”

除了便利的手机支付，洛克觉得中国的交通也特别方便。“中国的国土面积那么大，就因为有四通八达的高铁网络，所以从一个地方到另外一个地方十分的方便快捷。”“我自己就喜欢搭乘高铁去不同的城市游玩，去探索不一样的中国。”

聊到中国最让他喜欢的东西，洛克不假

思索地回答，那就是中国的美食。“中国有太多美味的食物，平时出门逛街，只要见到没有吃过的美食，我都想要去尝试。不过这些食物当中，我最喜欢的还是饺子。”“我觉得饺子对中国人来说是一种特别重要的食物，更多时候，它代表了一种情怀。逢年过节，中国人就会吃饺子。在包饺子的过程中，全家人都会聚在一起，开开心心地参与，一家人其乐融融，非常让人羡慕。饺子这种看起来很简单的食物，背后却有着很深刻的意义，我认为非常难得。”洛克还回忆起自己被朋友邀请去他们家包饺子的经历，“一开始我完全不知道怎么包饺子，看别人包饺子好像也不是很难，我就想着把面皮捏起来就可以了……后来才发现，包饺子也有很多技巧。我学习了好久终于掌握了这些技巧，现在我自己也能包出比较像模像样的饺子了。”

回忆起自己在中国生活的多姿多彩的五年，洛克认为他之所以能够有这么多难忘的经历和体验，最重要的前提就是他愿意开口说话，愿意主动去和不同的人交流。“我最爱去城里瞎逛，去胡同里找小朋友们玩儿，教他们学英文，在街头找大爷们聊天儿，天南海北地唠嗑……”“我觉得我现在中文说得还不错，都是因为我愿意开口说话。我认为大家无论来自哪个国家，只要你愿意开口，通过交流就可以拉近彼此之间的距离。任何一个愿意主动交流的人都肯定会受益匪浅的。”

洛克如今很得意的一件事就是他交到了很多来自中国不同地方的朋友，学会了一些中国的方言。他最喜欢东北的方言。说话间，洛克当场给我们表演了一段：“干哈呢？——来，老弟，你瞅啥啊？——瞅你咋地？——你再瞅一个试试？——试试就试试。”还有最近网上很流行的一句广东话绕口令：“各个国家有各个国家的国歌。”广东话的不同声调他也能掌握得入木三分，说得有模有样。

“我想更多地了解中国，有机会我想去不同的城市看一看，去了解更多的中国文化。”说着，他还调皮地给我们比了一个心，“I Love China！中国，我爱你哦！”

Scan for a Video

献给南京的“情书”

A “Love Letter” to Nanjing

A "Love Letter" to Nanjing

Erica Felton is a beautiful blonde blue-eyed girl. She grew up in Nanjing where she received her senior secondary school education at an international school. After having lived for five years there, she left China to study at a university abroad. After one year, she returned because she missed the city very much. When she came back, she wanted to leave something for Nanjing. In the end, she decided to shoot a short film about Nanjing where she once lived as a special "love letter" dedicated to the city. Erica said that Nanjing felt like more of a hometown than a foreign land.

As a filmmaker, Erica has shot many films about cities and countries. She uses her camera to record her footprints wherever she goes. She knows that those films she shot when she was younger are by no means mature, and she continues to explore her own filmmaking style. But many people wondered why she hadn't shot a film about Nanjing, the city where she lived for five years. "That's the question I've been asking myself. It's where I grew up, spent five years. Why haven't I

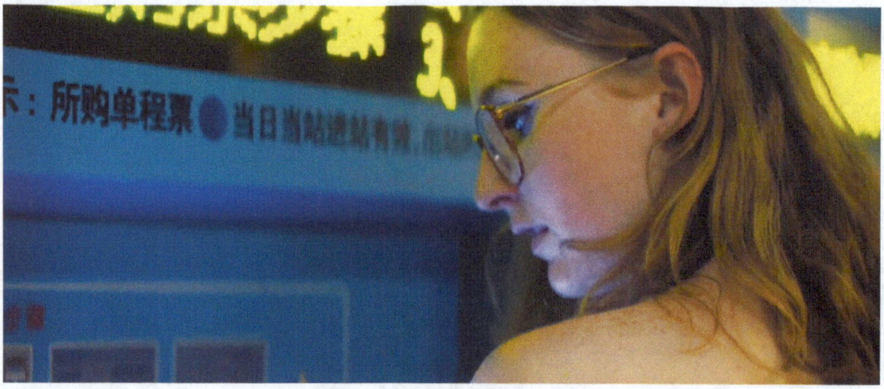

made a video? Actually, it's not that hard if I want to do it. Surely I have enough footage for it."

A year ago, Erica left Nanjing and everything she was familiar with. That was when she discovered the answer to this question. "After I left Nanjing, I realized that when you lived somewhere, you had no idea how you were going to be able to capture a city in its entirety, in the way that you saw it as your home. Do you take the touristy route and just show the overtly tourist destinations, or do you just show the mundane and hope people understand? It's very hard."

Erica had so much to say about China, especially Nanjing. But where could she start? There were so many thoughts in her mind. She decided to go out and see what she could find in the streets.

In the Nanjing Confucius Temple pedestrian street, Erica met a lovely girl who timidly came over to greet her and shyly asked if they could take a photo together. Erica readily agreed, hugging the little girl with a charming smile. After taking a few steps, she met another lady who politely asked if they could take a photo together. Later, a fashionable young lady walked nearby. All of them made this "bizarre" request without exception, but Erica always agreed readily. "I am happy to share this experience with you. In the streets of Nanjing, every couple of minutes, oh that's an exaggeration, every now and then, you get stopped and asked for a photo. That's mad, isn't it? That's just bizarre. I'm happy to do it. After I left Nanjing, whenever I thought of China, such scenes always appeared before my eyes. Who can forget such happy encounters?"

While wondering through the streets of Nanjing, Erica's eyes reflected endless memories. "If you asked me to make this video five years ago, I think I would have described the city as busy and crazy. But now I think differently. Nanjing is vibrant and crazy, but it is also tranquil and harmonious. In my memory, there are many tiny moments which slip away inadvertently and are so precious. It's scary trying to be able to capture somewhere and do it justice in the video. And I don't even know I could do it here. But I'm going to try. It's really hard. I think I romanticize Nanjing in my head. But then again, who doesn't romanticize their childhoods? I look back at Nanjing with complete and utter fondness, and unadulterated love for Nanjing, honestly. Wherever I am, my love for Nanjing does not change."

After she returned to Nanjing a year later, Erica found it both familiar and strange. "During the five years I lived in Nanjing, I walked through all the streets of the city, and thought that I knew everything here. But when I came back this time, I found that so many incredible things were happening." When Erica came back, she was shocked by the changes she saw. Countless new buildings were springing up, and the urban infrastructure had been updated. The vacant lot she remembered has become a business district with crisscrossing streets. Many things are changing fast in this world, especially in China. Nanjing, the ancient capital of six dynasties, is glowing with new vitality. In Nanjing, history and modernity quietly blend, and the collision of tradition and modernity is fascinating.

"I think coming back for a while after being away for a year or so made me realize life definitely moves on when you're gone and things change. And you got to appreciate what you once had. That's how I won't let down my love for this city," she says emotionally.

"In this film, I don't want you to listen to me waxing poetic about life and about Nanjing, and about how much I yearn for the past, because that's not what I want this to be. Nanjing was a home that I once lived in. I love dearly for all its quirks and its weird moments. How beautiful it could be. And I genuinely with all of my heart miss it. But I am glad that I can go back and witness what I used to be surrounded by, and that I appreciated that from afar when I left. I want to dedicate this film as a 'love letter' to Nanjing, the city I used to call home. I love Nanjing!"

献给南京的“情书”

艾丽卡·菲尔顿是一位金发碧眼的大美女，她从小生活在南京，高中时期就读于南京的国际学校，在南京生活了五年之后，她离开中国去国外读大学。在与南京阔别一年之后，基于对这个城市的无尽思念，她再一次回到了这里。这一次回来，她想为南京留下些什么。最终，她决定拍摄一部有关南京的短片，来介绍这座她曾经生活、居住过的城市，作为她献给南京的一封特殊的“情书”。艾丽卡说，南京于她，是他乡，更是故乡。

作为一名电影制作人，艾丽卡·菲尔顿曾经拍摄过一系列有关城市/国家的电影，她喜欢每到一个地方，就用镜头记录下她的

足迹。那些她少时的生涩之作，她明白还有很多不成熟的地方，她也一直在电影制作的道路上探索自己的定位。但有很多人好奇的是，对于南京——这个她曾经生活了五年的城市，为何她却一直没有制作一辑有关南京的电影呢？"这个问题，我也一直在问我自己。我在南京生活了五年，这个城市到处都留下了我成长的印记。可是我却一直都没有做成电影。我为什么没有去做呢？"艾丽卡微笑着说，"其实只要我想去做，这并不是一件难事，对于南京，我肯定有满满的影片素材。"

直到一年前艾丽卡离开了南京，离开了她所熟悉的一切，这个问题才有了答案。"离开南京之后我才认识到，当你真正身居一个城市时，你是无法简单地把一个城市所有的样貌展现出来的。就好像南京，我视南京如家一样珍贵。如果我要拍摄一部有关南京的电影，我是跟随着南京的旅游路线，专门讲解拍摄一些南京热门的旅游景点，还是单纯记录南京人平凡的一天，然后期待那些从未来过南京的观众可以明白这些？对我来说，这真的太难了。”

对于中国，特别是对于南京，艾丽卡有太多的话想说，太多的内容想要表达。但又该从哪里开始说起呢？艾丽卡的大脑里千头万绪，太多的想法都急于喷涌而出。她决定索性直接出门，看看在南京的大街小巷上能遇上些什么有趣的事情。

在南京夫子庙步行街，艾丽卡遇到了一位可爱的小姑娘，小姑娘怯生生地上前和她打招呼，羞涩地询问是否可以和她合影。艾丽卡爽快地答应了，搂着小姑娘露出了迷人的微笑。没走几步，她又遇到了一位女士，也礼貌地要求合影。后来，旁边又走来一位时髦的姑娘……大家都无一例外提出了这个“奇怪”的请求，艾丽卡却毫不见怪地一一允诺。“这件事情是我很乐意和大家分享的。在南京街头，每隔几分钟——可能有点儿夸张，反正时不时的，总会有人叫住我想要和我合影。我总觉得不可思议，很神奇，当然我也很乐意这么做。当我离开之后，每当我想起中国，这样的场景总会浮现在我的眼前。谁能忘记这样的奇遇呢？”

漫步在南京的大街小巷，艾丽卡的眼神里流露出无尽的回忆。"如果让我五年前来做这个电影，我想那时的我一定会把这里描述成一个忙碌而且疯狂的城市。但现在我的想法完全不同了。南京这个城市有着充满活力和疯狂的一面，但它也有安静祥和的另外一面。在我的记忆中，有很多微小的瞬间，很多不经意就会溜走的瞬间，是那么的珍贵，我好想把它们记录下来。但有时我也会感到害怕，我很害怕以我个人的视角不能客观公正地将我对这个城市的看法表达出来。因为这对我来说真的很难，我担心我会把南京描述得太浪漫了，但我想无论是谁，都会把自己喜爱的东西浪漫化的。我是那么的喜爱南京，每次回忆起南京，我的心里都充满了对这个城市的无限喜欢。无论我在哪里，我对南京的喜爱都未曾改变过。”

一年之后重返南京，对艾丽卡·菲尔顿来说，这个城市既熟悉又陌生。“我在南京生活的那五年，走遍了南京的大街小巷，我一直以为，我对南京的一切都很熟悉。但这一次回来，我发现，有太多不可思议的事情正在这个城市里悄然发生着。”艾丽卡刚回来的时候，对眼前的变化感到无比的震惊，无数新的高楼正在这个城市不断地出现，城市的建设也在不断更新。她记忆中原本没有人烟的空地，转眼间就变成了街道纵横的商业区。在这个世界上，很多东西都在飞速更迭着，尤其是在中国。南京这个曾经的六朝古都正焕发出新的生机。在南京，历史和现代可以融合得不动声色，传统和现代的碰撞是那样的令人着迷。

“这一次我重回旧地，最大的感悟就是——当你离开某个地方，生活并不会因为你的离开而停止。很多事情、很多地方都会改变，因此我更要珍惜曾经拥有过的一切，才不辜负我对这个城市的热爱。"艾丽卡感慨地说。

"在这个电影中，我不想太过矫情地一直念叨我对南京生活的想念，也不想一直缅怀过去。南京是我曾经的家。我真切地喜爱这里，喜欢这里的人，喜欢这里的食物，喜欢在这里发生的奇怪又可爱的际遇，我能想象的最美好的生活也不过如此。我很开心能够回到这里，再次亲眼看一看曾经环绕着我的一切，我真心地感恩这一切。我想将这部电影作为'情书'献给南京，这个我曾经称之为家的地方。我爱南京！"

Scan for a Video

蒙古女孩的广州生活

Mongolian Girl's Life in Guangzhou

Mongolian Girl's Life in Guangzhou

In front of the iconic arched gate of Jinan University in Guangzhou, we met a beautiful, fashionable girl. At first glance, her clothing style was no different from any ordinary Guangzhou girl. She stood at the school gate, who has big beautiful eyes and slightly curly hair, waving to us and greeting us with a smile. Once she said, "Sainuu", you felt her unique exotic charm. She is Batbayar Uyunbilig (Батбаяр Оюунбилэг), a Mongolian girl from Erdenet, Mongolia.

She has been living and studying in China for four years. Two years ago she was admitted to Jinan University, and thus began her colorful university life in Guangzhou. "My life at Jinan University is really enriched and interesting. In addition to attending classes, there are many fun club activities. I signed up for the university art troupe to learn Chinese dancing." Many styles of Chinese dancing, which are different from the lively, enthusiastic style of Mongolian dancing, emphasize both strength and softness as well as the combination of movement and tranquility. This is attractive and challenging for

Batbayar, who is good at singing and dancing. "Learning Chinese dancing has helped me make many new Chinese friends, and I've learned more about Chinese culture through dancing. I'm enjoying this experience very much."

In her spare time, Batbayar likes to read in the university library. "I like to go to the library and read books about the history of Guangzhou." Guangzhou is an ancient city with a history of over one thousand years, and she is attracted to its unique Cantonese culture and cuisine. "I can learn a lot of interesting history and stories about Guangzhou through books. When I read these stories, it makes me wish I could be there to see it with my own eyes." Every holiday she likes to leave the campus and wander around downtown Guangzhou, looking for what she read about in the books. "The subway in Guangzhou is very convenient. It can take me to every corner of the city. I love taking the subway. There are all kinds of people there. Their hurried steps and different voices are representative of Guangzhou. There are so many beautiful scenic spots in Guangzhou. Day or night, you can discover the charm of this city anywhere." She likes to walk around and take pictures with her SLR camera under the Guangzhou Tower, on Baiyun Mountain, by the Pearl River and near the Liede Bridge.... She uses her camera to capture and feel every bit of the city.

Beijing Road and Shangxiajiu Pedestrian Street in Guangzhou are her favorite places. "On Beijing Road which is the birthplace of Guangzhou, you can see the ruins of historical monuments with a long history of two thousand years. Through these ruins, I can see the development and enduring prosperity of Guangzhou." Beijing Road is

a large business district in downtown Guangzhou, and a place where many centuries-old, time-honored shops still operate and thrive. "I like the food along Beijing Road, including Guangzhou's steamed rice rolls, beef offal, desserts, and stews. There are so many kinds of delicious food." While talking about the city's delicious food, Batbayar's eyes sparkle with excitement. "The last time I went to the Lin Heung Tea House on Beijing Road, I tasted so many delicious dim sum such as ham cookies, sweet heart pastries, and lotus paste moon cakes. It makes me think that it would be great if my family could come to China. They have never been to China before, and have not had the chance to taste the delicious food in Guangzhou. I think that my grandmother will love the food here."

"There are a lot to see in the pedestrian street. I have seen all kinds of folk art, like animal figures woven with tree leaves. The craftsman can weave a lifelike cricket with just some ordinary grass and tree leaves. It's really amazing!" While talking about the fun things she discovered, she was excited. "I saw a folk artist playing a very special musical instrument I had never seen before. He played so beautifully that I couldn't help but stand there and listen for a long time."

Although her life in China is never dull, Batbayar still misses her family far away. Her hometown, Erdenet, is Mongolia's third largest city in northern Mongolia and the capital of Orhon Province. It has a temperate continental climate, with the coldest January temperature averaging minus 17°C. "I finally went home for New Year's Day last year. It is 2,986 kilometers from Guangzhou. Although there is no time difference, the trip spans the four seasons. There is no winter in Guangzhou. I haven't lived through a real winter for several years. Returning home for New Year's Day, I felt the real winter again."

Speaking of that trip back home, Batbayar's eyes reflects great nostalgia. "I brought my family some dim sum from the Lin Heung Tea House in Guangzhou. They all loved my gifts." Erdenet had a very strong New Year festive atmosphere. The whole family happily got together and ate Mongolian traditional New Year's food and sang and danced to celebrate the New Year. The Guangzhou specialty products she brought to her family also made them feel very happy. Batbayar's parents have never been to China. "When I have the chance, I will take my family to visit China, especially Guangzhou, and enjoy the delicious food here." Batbayar is looking forward to this.

"China is changing with each passing day. Chinese cities are booming, and Chinese people are kind and friendly. There are so many stories in China to discover and so many places I will explore. I love China, and my story about China will continue."

蒙古女孩的广州生活

在暨南大学最具标志性的大拱门前，我们见到了那位漂亮、时尚的姑娘。乍一看，她的衣着打扮与普通的广州女孩没有什么区别，一头微曲秀发的她笑吟吟地站在校门口和我们挥手打着招呼，那双漂亮有神的大眼睛闪动着灵动的光亮。“sainuu!”她一开口，就能感受到她身上独特的异国风情和魅力，她就是来自蒙古国额尔登特的蒙古女孩巴特巴雅尔·乌云毕力格（БатбаярОюунбилэг）。

今年是乌云毕力格在中国学习、生活的第四年。两年前她考上了暨南大学，从此开启了她在广州丰富多彩的大学生活。“在暨南大学的学习、生活实在太丰富、太有趣了，除了上课，还有好多好玩儿的社团活动。我报名参加了学校艺术团，学习中国舞蹈。”与蒙古舞蹈节奏明快、热情奔放的风格截然不同，中国舞蹈更讲究刚柔并济、动静结合，这对能歌善舞的乌云毕力格来说，既是吸引，也是挑战。“学习中国舞蹈不仅让我认识了

很多中国朋友，也让我通过舞蹈更了解中国文化，我很享受这个过程。”

忙碌的学习之余，乌云毕力格最爱去学校的图书馆待着。“我好喜欢去图书馆翻阅一些有关广州历史的书籍。”广州是个有着千年历史的古城，独特的广府文化和美食深深吸引着乌云毕力格。“在书中，我可以了解到很多有关广州的有趣的历史和故事。看书的时候我总在想，如果我能亲眼去看一看有多好。”所以每到假期，乌云毕力格就爱离开校园，去广州市区到处走走，去寻找那些书上所记载的内容。“广州的地铁非常的便捷，地铁可以带我去到广州的各个角

落。”“我很喜欢乘地铁，地铁站里形形色色的人们，匆匆的脚步，不同的口音……这些就是最地道、最真实的广州。”乌云毕力格笑着说，“广州有太多美丽的风景。无论白天还是夜晚，在广州的各个角落，你都能发现这个城市的迷人之处。”所以，她最爱带着单反相机，四处走走拍拍。广州塔下，白云山上，珠江边，猎德大桥旁……处处都留下了她的美丽身影。她用相机去记录、用心去体会和感受这座城市的点点滴滴。

广州的北京路、上下九步行街是她最爱逛的地方。“在北京路，广州这个城市最早开始的地方，可以看到有着悠久历史的千年古道遗迹，我喜欢透过遗迹去感受广州城两千年来的发展和繁华。”北京路作为广州市中心较大的商业区，是广州百年老店和老字号商铺的集中地，这里店铺众多，规模较大，商业兴旺。“我喜欢北京路上的美食，广州的肠粉、牛杂、甜品、炖品……简直有太多数不尽的美味。”谈到广州的美食，她的眼睛闪烁着兴奋的光芒，“上一次我去北京路上的莲香楼，品尝到了好多美味的点心，比如鸡仔饼、老婆饼、莲蓉月饼……当时我就在想，如果我的家人也能来中国有多好，他们从未来过中国，也从未有机会品尝到广州的美食，我相信我的奶奶一定会喜欢这里的食物的。”

“步行街上还有好多有趣的存在，我见过用树叶编织的各种各样的动物。手工艺人只用普普通通的几根草和叶子就可以编织出一只栩栩如生的蟋蟀，实在太厉害了！”聊到好玩儿有趣的发现，乌云毕力格止不住兴奋，“还有一些民间艺人，在路边吹着一种很特殊的乐器，我从来没有见过那样的乐器，但他的演奏很动听，我忍不住站在那里听了好久。”

虽然在中国的生活多姿多彩，但乌云毕力格仍会时常想念远在家乡的亲人。她的家乡——额尔登特，是蒙古国的第三大城市，位于蒙古国的北部，也是鄂尔浑省首府。那里属于温带大陆性气候，最冷的一月份的平

均气温可以达到零下17°C。“去年新年我终于回家了。从广州到我的家乡，相距2986公里。虽然没有昼夜相隔，但却跨越了四季。广州一年四季没有冬天，我好多年没有经历过真正的冬天了。回家过新年，我可以重新去感受一个纯粹的冬天。”

说到那一次的回乡之旅，乌云毕力格的目光中流露出无限的怀念和期待。“我给家人们带去了广州莲香楼的小点心，我这份跨越了2986公里的礼物，他们都特别喜欢。”过年时候的额尔登特有着非常浓厚的新年气氛，全家人团聚在一起，品尝着蒙古国传统的新年食物，载歌载舞庆祝新年。她给家人们带去的广州特产，也让家人们觉得非常幸福。乌云毕力格的父母从未来过中国。“有机会我一定要带我的家人们来中国看看，特别是来广州，带他们好好品尝广州的美食。”乌云毕力格满心期待着。

“中国的变化日新月异，中国的城市蓬勃发展，中国的人民善良友好。中国有太多故事等待我去发现，有太多地方值得我去探索。我爱中国，我和中国的故事还会一直延续。”

Scan for a Video

祝您用餐愉快
Enjoy Your Meal
美团外卖

Enjoy Your Meal

"Make a phone call and later knock on the door to introduce yourself and have a polite, confident smile. It is essential to check all the items before delivery, and it is very important to present them with both hands." It was around 10 am, and dozens of delivery boys from the Meituan Wudaokou Food Takeout Delivery Team were receiving their morning training. Team leader Zhang Hui was leading them in familiarizing themselves with the steps of food takeout delivery services. Among them, a young foreigner attracted everyone's attention. He is Raz Galor from Israel, an international student at Peking University. His Chinese name is Gao Yousi.

"The food delivery service industry in China is amazing. Delivery boys can deliver food in half an hour. This speed is really amazing." To better understand this industry and gain first-hand experience as a delivery boy in China, Gao Yousi applied for the job as a delivery

boy. After the platform examined and approved his application, he was ready to begin work.

Today is his first day, and after everything was ready he began to take orders. At first, he was not familiar with the software and the process of receiving orders. His first order was far away, and he was half an hour late. The customer didn't give him a negative review, but coldly took the delivery and indifferently closed the door without looking at him or thanking him. This made Gao Yousi feel very upset and frustrated, and he felt a bit sad and said, "The customer seemed dissatisfied with me, and I was also dissatisfied with myself." But he soon cheered up and received the next order.

After finishing a few more orders, he gradually got the hang of it, and even began to learn from other delivery boys on how to receive multiple orders at a time. "Enjoy your meal," he said, happily delivering his good wishes to a customer. When a customer was satisfied with his delivery service, he felt very pleased. "When I communicate with customers, see their satisfactory smile and hear them thank me, I feel

that my hard work is worthwhile." While waiting for more orders, he said emotionally, "So far, I am keenly aware that the takeout delivery business is not easy at all. It requires a high IQ and a strong ability to learn and respond quickly. Delivery boys often receive many orders at the same time, and they need to make quick decisions to arrange the routes to pick up and deliver the food to customers in the shortest time."

After working hard in the morning, he was finally able to sit down and have lunch. Other delivery boys told him that a delivery boy usually completes at least 40 orders a day. But this morning, Gao Yousi only completed six orders. In the afternoon and evening, he would have to finish 34 orders, and this was making him extremely stressed.

That evening, all the delivery boys were very busy receiving orders during peak hours, as was Gao Yousi. By this time, however, he was able to handle the orders much better. He received his orders on the mobile phone platform, and he planned time-saving routes. He was able to find residences, office buildings, shopping malls or some strange places according to the map, and made his deliveries on time. He got used to running while on foot. Some locations were in old apartments with no elevators, so he sometimes had to run up to the sixth floor. There were also some office buildings where delivery boys were not allowed to enter, so he had to wait in the cold wind for customers to come out to get the food.

It was getting dark and the temperature was dropping. Like countless other food delivery boys, Gao Yousi was running all around the city.

Suddenly he received a very special order. After he hurried to deliver the takeout, he found that it was his father who had placed the order. His father knew that he worked as a delivery boy today, so he wrote down Gao Yousi's employee number in advance and designated him to finish the order. This embarrassed but also moved Gao Yousi. Although he made the delivery, he didn't have time to rest and talk with his father because it would make him late for his next order.

For his first day, Gao Yousi worked from 10 am to 10 pm, finished 17 orders and earned a total of 80 yuan. In Beijing, the record number of orders completed by a delivery boy is 84. Many delivery boys receive more than 40 orders a day, and their average monthly salary is 6,500-8,500 yuan. "I didn't expect that delivering takeout would require abilities and skills," Gao Yousi says emotionally. On the way home after work, he saw many delivery boys still standing in the cold wind, waiting to deliver midnight snacks. "I thought Israelis loved their jobs," he says, "but today I realized that Chinese people are the most hard-working in the world."

Later, he talked with some of the delivery boys. "The food takeout delivery industry in foreign countries is completely different from

China. They don't have as many choices included in the software as China does. There are very few dishes available, and most

orders are placed by a phone call, which is very backward. Also, the delivery takes a long time: it takes at least one hour for the food to come to your home, so it is cold when it arrives. Moreover, foreign delivery boys will charge customers a tip of 10 or 15 percent. After experiencing the work today, I admire you from the bottom of my heart. Chinese delivery boys are really amazing." Team leader Zhang Hui said emotionally, "Many people still don't know much about our industry. When we receive orders, we are responsible for finishing them. The work is indeed very exhausting. Sometimes we encounter difficulties. If we fail to deliver orders on time, we hope that customers can understand. During winter, the number of delivery boys will decrease, but the number of orders will increase sharply, which puts a lot of pressure on us."

Through this special experience, Gao Yousi came to understand the hard-working spirit of the Chinese people. "It is no wonder that only in China can such an industry thrive," he said. He said that by seeing the hard work of the Chinese people, as well as their efficiency, conscientious, and responsible attitude, he had come to realize that China's rapid development cannot be separated from the unremitting efforts of these ordinary Chinese people.

"Chinese delivery boys don't give up easily. Their incomes are determined by how many orders they complete. As a customer, we order and pick up our takeout food with ease, but it is these delivery boys who keep running and running, exchanging their sweat for a respectable income. Please value their hard work!"

祝您用餐愉快

“敲门致电要礼貌，自信微笑来介绍。核对单品不可少，双手呈递很重要。”北京时间上午十点左右，美团五道口外送组几十个外卖小哥正在进行集训。组长张辉正带领着大家一起熟悉他们的送餐服务步骤。在这当中，一位外国小伙子特别吸引大家的注意。他就是北京大学的留学生，来自以色列的高佑思。

“中国的外卖服务实在太神奇了，只要手机上下单，外卖小哥在半小时之内就能将外卖送到我们手上，这个速度实在令人惊

叹。”为了更好地了解外卖这个行业，近距离体验中国外卖小哥一天的生活，高佑思在平台申请成为一名外卖小哥，经过平台审核通过之后他就可以正式接单了。

今天是他成为外卖小哥的日子。在一切都准备就绪之后，高佑思开始接单了。由于一开始不熟悉软件的运用和接单的流程，他有些手忙脚乱。再加上第一单路途较远，他迟到了整整半个小时才将外卖送到顾客手中。虽然顾客并没有给差评，但看都不看他一眼，也没有说声感谢，就冷漠地接过外卖关上了门。这让高佑思感到十分懊恼和挫败。“好像顾客对我有一点儿不满，我对自己也非常不满意。”高佑思有点儿难过地说。不

过很快他就打起精神开始接下一单。

送了几单之后，高佑思渐渐找到了感觉，他甚至开始学习其他外卖小哥，尝试一次接多个订单。“祝您用餐愉快！”每送完一单，高佑思都会愉快地向顾客送出祝福。每遇到一个对他的服务表示满意的顾客，他都觉得特别开心。“每当和顾客沟通，看到他们满意的笑容，听到他们对我的感谢，我就会觉得一切的辛苦都值得。”在等单的间隙，高佑思感慨地说，“到目前为止，我深刻地认识到一点——送外卖一点儿都不容易。它需要很高的智商、很强的学习能力和快速反应能力。外卖员经常会同时收到很多个单子，他们需要做出非常快速的决定，安排好最省时的取菜、送菜的路线，这样才能在最短的时间内将外卖送到顾客手中。”

辛辛苦苦一上午，高佑思终于可以坐下来吃午饭了。其他外卖小哥告诉他，一般一个外卖小哥一天的送单量至少是40单。但一个上午，高佑思才送了6单。所以，下午和晚上，他还要完成34单，这让他感到压力山大。

傍晚时分，是外卖订单的晚高峰时期。高佑思开始接到源源不断的订单。这时候的他也已经得心应手了许多。手机平台接单，去商家取订单，规划好省时的路线，无论是居民楼、办公楼、商场，还是其他奇奇怪怪的地方，他都能根据地图顺利地找到，并准时将外卖送达。在这个城市里，他已经渐渐习惯了一路奔跑着前进。有的送餐地点在老旧的居民楼，那里没有电梯，他只能徒步跑上六楼；有的办公楼不允许外卖小哥进入，他只好在寒风中等着顾客出来拿外卖。

天渐渐黑了，气温越来越低。高佑思仍和无数的外卖小哥一样，在这个城市中一路飞奔着，争分夺秒。这天晚上，他接到了很特殊的一单，等他辛苦送到后才发现点单的竟然是他的爸爸。原来，爸爸知道他今天要当外卖小哥，所以提前记下来他的工号，指定让他送过来。这让高佑思又尴尬又感动。虽然遇见爸爸，但他也没有时间停下来休息一会儿和爸爸多聊几句，因为他的下一单要迟到了。

这一整天外卖小哥的工作，高佑思从上午十点忙到晚上十点，才完成了17单，总共赚到了80块钱。而北京单王每天的送单数是84单，其他的外卖员每天接单平均在40单以上，每月能拿到的平均工资为6500～8500元。高佑思不禁感叹：“没想到送外卖也需要那么多的能力和技巧。”在结束工作回去的路上，高佑思看到还有很多外卖小哥仍在寒风中站着等着送宵夜。“我本来以为以色列人很热爱工作，但今天我才发现，其实中国人才是全世界最拼、最努力的一个民族。”

高佑思走到外卖小哥们中间和他们聊起了天。“国外的外卖行业和中国完全不同，不会像中国的外卖软件那样覆盖很多选择，国外能选的菜很少，而且大多都是打电话下单，非常落后。国外的外卖小哥送外卖的速度非常慢，饭菜送到你家的时间至少是一小时，一般饭菜送到的时候都已经凉了。而且国外的外卖小哥还会向顾客收取10%或者15%的小费。经过今天的体验，我从内心里佩服你们。中国的外卖小哥实在太了不起了。”组长张辉感慨地说：“现在可能还有很多人不太了解我们这个行业。对我们外卖员来说，当一个订单到我们手上之后，我们就要对这个订单负责。外卖行业确实是蛮辛苦的，有些时候，迫不得已遇到各种状况，订单超时了，还希望顾客能够多理解。到了冬天，外卖员的数量会减少，但是外卖的订单数量却会激增，这对我们外卖员来说也是很大的压力……”

通过这一次特别的体验，高佑思深刻地感受到中国人吃苦耐劳的精神。他感叹道：“怪不得只有在中国这片土地上，外卖这样的行业才能蓬勃发展。”中国人对努力和效率的追求，对工作的认真负责，让他深刻地

认识到，中国的高速发展离不开这些普通中国人的不懈努力。

“中国的外卖小哥不会轻易放弃自己的顾客，他们送多少单，就有多少收入。在我们轻松点餐和取餐之间，是这些外卖小哥不断地奔跑奔跑再奔跑，用自己的汗水换得一份值得尊敬的收入。还请多多珍惜他们的努力！”

Scan for a Video

跟着 Trix 一起认识北京

Getting to Know More about Beijing with Trix

Getting to Know More about Beijing with Trix

Although Beijing is cold in the winter, there is warmth every morning. The breakfast joint in the Shijia Hutong near Chaoyangmen Street in Dongcheng District gives off hot steam. The old men and women walking nearby exhale warm air, and even the tinkling bells of bicycles brim with joy. Appearing in the hutong is a pretty girl with a dark complexion and shoulder-length slightly curly hair. She is wearing a black cotton jacket with a lovely pattern, and she smiles sweetly. Her eyes light up when she sees the big, glistening sugar-coated haws. She can't wait to buy one and nibble at it with smiles of satisfaction and enjoyment. This girl intoxicated by the delicious sugar-coated haw is Trix Ingado from Africa.

Trix is from Nairobi, Kenya, one of the most fashionable and modern cities in Africa. She is a journalist for KTN News. She came to China

in 2018 through the China-Africa Press Exchange Center's program which invites foreigners to China to gain first-hand China experience for themselves, and helps them understand China from political, economic and cultural perspectives. Trix believes that her trip is fulfilling as it helps her better understand China. As a journalist, therefore, she can better inform her readers about China.

After eating the sugar-coated haw, Trix arrives at her destination: the Shijia Hutong Museum, located in the Shijia Hutong in Dongcheng District, Beijing, and the first hutong museum in Beijing. It displays miniature replicas of 130 courtyards and also objects used by Chinese people and some old photos. The word "hutong" first appeared during the Yuan Dynasty (1206-1368), and is used to describe the smaller streets in Beijing connecting people's homes. There are many traditional homes in Beijing's hutongs called *siheyuan* (courtyard homes). The Shijia Hutong Museum used to be the *siheyuan* of Ling Shuhua, a well-known Chinese female writer. Trix loves the hutongs in Beijing, and she watched documentaries about them before coming to China. She believes that the hutongs showcase the old lifestyle of Beijing residents and represent China's history along with the Great Wall and the Forbidden City.

She enters the museum and sees old objects like a bicycle with wheels 28 inches in diameter, an enamel basin, a copper glass-covered kerosene lamp and a decorated wooden dressing mirror. She examines old photos depicting the past lives of Chinese people such as soldiers sewing buttons in their spare time, people saluting a photo of Chairman Mao, and children making snowmen in the winter. To Trix, the charm of Beijing is not only in its modernity, but also in its ancient elements. In this city which combines the past with the present, Trix feels Beijing's charm and also its profound historical impact.

After visiting the museum, Trix invites Chinese friends to eat Chinese food. In her opinion, Chinese food is very rich, and quite different from African food. She likes to eat pork fillets with sweet and sour sauce, prawns with sauce, twice-cooked pork slices, stir-fried shredded pork with bamboo shoots, and many other dishes whose names she doesn't know. To her, Chinese food is rich and delicious. Because she spends most of her time in Beijing, one of Trix's favorite and most frequently eaten dishes is Beijing roast duck. Beijing roast duck is served in slices, with golden, oily and crispy skin, and plump and soft meat. When you pick up the slices and put them on the thin pancake, along with the side ingredients and

sauce, you will enjoy a treat. Trix likes to dip the duck slices in sugar and eat it in her own unique and delicious way. "I love Chinese food!" Trix says contentedly after lunch.

When talking about her life in Beijing, Trix, like many foreigners, is deeply impressed with one particular point: like other Chinese cities, Beijing has a particularly well-developed e-commerce infrastructure. Almost all places support payments by mobile phone, from large supermarkets to small stores in the streets. JD.com, Taobao.com, and various e-commerce platforms make life easier for Chinese people. "You can buy anything you want," Trix says happily. As she speaks, she shows off her black cotton jacket. She quickly takes it off and turns it inside out, and it becomes a red cotton jacket. This jacket can be worn on both sides, and looks like two pieces of clothing. Trix bought it for only 89 yuan on Taobao. Her jacket is very warm and comfortable, and can withstand the cold wind in Beijing, which makes her especially happy because she thinks she got more than she had paid for. Trix also shows off the African-style golden necklace she bought on Taobao. When she saw this piece of jewelry, she was astonished. Trix didn't expect to buy inexpensive African-style jewelry in China, but many customers posted positive reviews saying they liked the necklace. Trix thinks that China's developed e-commerce not only makes life easier for Chinese people, but also brings closer Chinese culture and the cultures of the rest of the world, and enables diverse cultures to appreciate one another.

Finally, Trix arrives at Sanlitun, one of the most expensive business districts in Beijing. With modern high-rise buildings, bustling crowds, and all kinds of goods, Sanlitun is full of vigor and vitality. The reason why Trix likes Sanlitun so much is that it represents the international, modern and inclusive elements of Beijing. In Sanlitun, there are people from all over the world, who live their own lives with their own different jobs, and they are not rejected just because they are foreigners. This is exactly how Trix feels about Beijing and China. Although people look different and have different diets and living habits, they are all striving to live happy lives. Beijing not only has a historic past, but also an inclusive, open and modern present. Trix is trying to embrace this characteristic of Beijing, a city which combines modern and ancient elements, and she is constantly learning more about it through her experience gained by living here.

跟着 Trix 一起认识北京

北京的冬天虽然冷，但每一个早上都是热腾腾的。东城区朝阳门街道史家胡同的早餐店冒着热腾腾的烟火气，早起遛弯的大爷大妈嘴里呼着热气，就连“丁零零”的自行车都呼喊着快活的气息。一个穿着有可爱图案的黑棉服、肤色黝黑靓丽、及肩的秀发散着小波浪卷、笑起来甜甜的女孩出现在了胡同里。看见个头儿顶大、亮晶晶的糖葫芦时，她的眼睛也亮了，迫不及待地买了一支，一口咬下去，露出满意而享受的笑容。这个沉醉在美味糖葫芦里的女孩就是来自非洲的 Trix Ingado。

Trix 来自非洲肯尼亚的内罗毕，非洲最时尚、最现代化的城市之一。她是 KTN 新闻的一名记者，在 2018 年，她通过中非新闻交流中心的项目来到中国。这个项目主要是邀请外国人来中国亲身体验和感受中国，从政治、经济、文化多个角度了解中国。Trix 坚信自己这一趟来得很值，因为她可以真正地认识中国，也可以作为一名记者让更多的人跟着她认识中国。

吃完糖葫芦，Trix也走到了她今天的目的地——史家胡同博物馆。史家胡同博物馆位于北京东城区的史家胡同，是北京首家胡同博物馆，里面复原、陈列了130个院落的微缩模型和中国人使用过的物件及一些老照片。“胡同”是元代以来北京地区对比较小的街道的称呼，它往往连接着居民的住宅。北京的胡同里有很多北京传统的房屋形式——四合院。史家胡同博物馆原本就是中国非常著名的女作家凌淑华居住过的四合院。Trix非常喜欢北京的胡同，她在来中国之前就看过关于胡同的纪录片。她认为，胡同体现的是北京人过去的生活方式，和长城、故宫一起代表着中国的历史和过去。当她走

进史家胡同博物馆时，二八式自行车、搪瓷盆、铜铸玻璃罩煤油灯、裱花的木制梳妆镜等老式生活器具都让她觉得魅力无穷。那些展示过去中国人生活的老照片——战士们在闲时缝扣子、人们对着毛主席像敬礼、小孩子们在冬天堆雪人，都让Trix感到新鲜。在Trix看来，北京的魅力不仅仅在于它非常现代化，还在于它仍然具有旧时的元素，是一个混搭的城市。在这个混搭的城市里，Trix感受到了历史的沉淀和岁月的魅力。

参观完史家胡同博物馆后，Trix约了中国朋友一起吃中国菜。在Trix眼里，中国菜实在是太丰富了，和非洲菜很不一样。糖醋里脊、浇汁大虾、回锅肉、笋片炒肉丝，还有许多她叫不出名字的菜，她都喜欢吃。对她来说，中国的食物丰富又美味。不过，由于大部分时间待在北京，Trix最喜欢、最常吃的一道名菜还是北京烤鸭。北京烤鸭上桌的时候被片成了一片片的，鸭皮金黄流油、酥脆可口，鸭肉饱满柔软。把它们夹起来放在薄如蝉翼的饼子上，加上小菜和酱，吃起来格外满足。Trix喜欢用烤鸭蘸白糖吃，吃法独特又美味。吃过午饭后，Trix 满足地说："我喜欢中国食物！"

说起在北京的交流生活，Trix 和很多外国人一样，印象最深的一点就是：北京和中国其他城市一样，电子商务特别发达——出门坐车，只要用手机刷一下就能够顺利上车而不需要刷卡；大到大型超市，小到街边小店，几乎所有的地方都能支持手机支付；京东、淘宝，各种各样的电商平台方便了普通人的生活。Trix 开心地说："想买什么都能买到。"说着，她展示了身上那件黑色的棉服。她迅速地脱下棉服，将衣服翻了个面，就变成了一件红色的棉服了。原来，这件棉服可以两面穿，看起来就像是两件衣服，Trix 在淘宝上只花了 89 元就买到了。衣服非常温暖舒服，完全可以抵御北京的寒风，这让她感觉"赚翻了"，特别幸福。Trix 还展示了具有非洲风格的金色项圈，这也是她在淘宝上购买的。当时看到这个饰品的时候，她觉得非常惊讶。Trix 没想到中国也能买到非洲风格的饰品，而且价格不贵，许多评价都表示很喜欢这个项圈。在 Trix 看来，中国发

达的电子商务不仅方便了中国人的生活，也让中国的文化和世界各地的文化更加紧密，更加能够互相欣赏。

最后，Trix 来到了三里屯。北京的三里屯是北京物价最高的商圈之一，非常繁华也十分受大家喜欢。时尚摩登的高楼大厦，熙熙攘攘的人群，各色各样的物品……三里屯洋溢着朝气和活力。Trix 非常喜欢三里屯的一点是，这里代表着北京最国际化、现代化和包容的一面。在三里屯，有来自全世界各个国家的人，他们各自过着自己的生活，从事着不同的职业，并没有因为是外国人就被排斥。这也正是北京乃至中国给 Trix 的感受。虽然大家的样貌、饮食、习惯各不相同，但大家都在努力地为幸福的生活奋斗。北京不仅有充满历史底蕴的过去，还有包容、开放、现代化的现在。Trix 正在努力拥抱着这样混搭的北京，不断地在生活经历中认识着北京。

Scan for a Video

在中国，生活可以这样精彩

An Exciting Life in China

An Exciting Life in China

Shenzhen is one of the most prosperous and fastest-growing cities in the world, and a Chinese city with many opportunities. Under the lush trees of a park in Shenzhen there are flat, clean pedestrian road. Early in the morning there are very few people in the park. When listening carefully, one can hear birds chirping and the faraway melodious music accompanying the elderly doing their exercises. A slender young man in a black T-shirt appears. He seems to be in his twenties, with curly, fluffy blonde hair and dressed very stylishly. He turns around. He is a white young man with deep eyes and a high nose. His name is Adam.

Born in a small town in Northern Ireland called Ballymena, Adam is 25 years old. He had a happy and free childhood playing music, football, and taking care of animals with his older brother. He didn't leave his hometown until he went to study at a university in Scotland, and after graduating he returned home to work. Despite his happy life

there, he was no longer satisfied with working and living in the same place he grew up, and wanted to see the world. Like all Internet savvy young people, his first thought was to search for a country with a rich culture and long history. China quickly appeared on screen. Seeking a more exciting life, he did not hesitate to apply for a visa. He then booked an air ticket and flew to Shenzhen, China. This is how Adam's colorful life in Shenzhen began.

It might be people's last guess that Adam, who looks more like a fashion trendsetter, came to Shenzhen to work as a primary school teacher. But he is quite satisfied with his job. Not only does it enable him to live a well-off life in Shenzhen, but it also exposes him to the lives of ordinary Chinese primary school students. This is so different from the childhood he and other children of his motherland experienced, which Adam finds very interesting. Of course, from his point of view, these kids are just as cute, passionate and positive as any child in the world, and being with them motivates him every day. Adam jokingly remarks, "This is the first job where I don't mind getting up early on Monday."

During holidays or breaks from work, Adam likes to travel to other parts of China. To Adam, China is a huge country, with great differences in geographical conditions and customs. During his two years working in Shenzhen, he has visited many parts of China. His favorite places are Yangshuo, Changsha and Guangzhou. Yangshuo is a county in Guangxi Zhuang Autonomous Region, and is known for its picturesque Lijiang River landscape. Changsha is the capital of Hunan Province, and has a long history and rich culture with such historical sites as the Mawangdui Han Tombs and Yuelu Academy. Guangzhou is the capital of Guangdong Province. It has a prosperous economy, beautiful flowers and delicious food. It is also a port city which has enjoyed enduring prosperity for more than two thousand years. These three places have different conditions and customs, but they are open and welcoming to visitors from all over the world. From Shenzhen it is also very convenient for Adam to travel abroad, especially to South and Southeast Asia. In just over two years, Adam has been to India, Sri Lanka, the Philippines, Malaysia, Indonesia, Cambodia and other countries. China was his destination for seeking an exciting life, and his starting point for exploring the wonderful surrounding regions.

Adam speaks very excitedly about the convenient and fun life here. Like many foreign friends who've come to China for the first time, Adam was amazed at the powerful functions of mobile phones. "In China, mobile phones are so powerful that you can do almost anything with them. If you need something, there's always an app which can help you find it." Adam likes to chat with his friends through WeChat, shop online at Taobao.com (the delivery of goods is amazingly fast), and pay his rent with a mobile phone app. When he goes out to take the bus or subway, he no longer needs to bring cash or a public transport card. Instead, he just opens a phone app and swipes it at the door.

But what gets Adam the most excited is when he talks about how he met his girlfriend. When he first came to Shenzhen, he was unfamiliar with everything. Through an Internet app he met Gail. They chatted, and fell in love at first sight after they met in person, just like the old Chinese saying, "A fated match across thousands of miles is bound by a thread." Adam and Gail have been living together for two years. They encourage and support each other, and even raise a dog named Bella who sleeps and snores like a pig. Adam's convenient and colorful life, and his ties of love in China, are a good example of how happiness is brought to ordinary people through technological innovations thanks to the rapid development of China's Internet over the past two decades. Here, everyone has the opportunity to enjoy the happiness of an innovative society.

To record his life in Shenzhen, Adam has shot short videos and posted them online, just like all young people around the world. He and his girlfriend have shot Chinese rap videos, China travel vlogs, imitation makeup videos, etc. The short video business in China is thriving, and Adam was found by some companies and program teams for a very special opportunity. Papitube is a multi-channel network founded by Papi Jiang, which is the online nickname of Jiang Yilei, one of China's most popular Internet celebrities, and her team. Papitube invited Adam to participate in a video blogger's event on a Hong Kong Cruise Line and at a video event in Beijing. Through this opportunity, Adam came

into contact with some of the best short video producers in China. In addition to this, he was invited to the Happy Camp TV show to sing and play games with many Chinese well-known stars. Happy Camp has been broadcast in China for 23 consecutive years, and it is one of the most popular variety shows with the highest ratings in China. As an ordinary young man, Adam never imagined he could live such an exciting and colorful life in China and be seen by so many Chinese people.

"These experiences are amazing," Adam says. "I never imaged these two years ago. I enjoy living in China every day, and I have no desire to go anywhere else." Everyone who has read Adam's story is convinced that his Chinese story is still continuing, and will get even more exciting in the future.

在中国，生活可以这样精彩

中国深圳，全世界最繁华、发展最快的城市之一，也是给予人最多机会的城市之一。深圳一处街心公园葱茏的树木掩映下是一条条铺设平整、干净的人行道。时间尚早，公园里人非常少，仔细聆听有鸟雀鸣叫的声音和远处伴随老人们锻炼的悠扬音乐声。一个身材修长、穿着黑色T恤的年轻人出现在公园里。他看上去二十多岁，顶着一头卷卷的、蓬松的金发，是当下流行的潮流青年的装扮。待他转过身来，才发现是位深目高鼻的白人小伙儿。他叫亚当。

亚当出生在北爱尔兰的小镇Ballymena，今年25岁了。亚当有一个快乐自由的童年，和哥哥一起玩乐器、踢足球、喂养小动物，打打闹闹开心地长大。直到读大学的时候，他才离开家乡去苏格兰学习，毕业后又回到了家乡工作。在快乐中长大的亚当已经不满足于只在家乡按部就班地工作、生活，他想要去看看更广阔、更丰富的世界。他和所有擅于运用互联网的年轻人一样，第一个想到的就是去网络上搜索文化丰富、历史悠久的国家。“中国”跃入了亚当的眼帘。为了寻找生活的精彩，他毫不迟疑地办理签证、订机票，飞到了中国深圳。亚当在深圳的精彩生活就这样开始了。

让人很难想象的是，看起来是时尚弄潮儿的亚当到深圳当了一名小学老师。亚当对

这份工作相当满意。因为这份工作不仅让他能够在深圳生活得比较宽裕，还让他接触到了中国普通小学生的生活。这和他所经历的童年和他祖国孩子们的童年差别很大，让他充满探索的乐趣。当然，在亚当看来，这些孩子和全世界所有的孩子一样活泼可爱、充满激情、积极向上，让他每天都朝气蓬勃。亚当开玩笑地说道：“这是第一份我不介意周一早起的工作。”

在做小学老师这份工作之余，亚当喜欢到处旅游。在亚当的眼里，中国地域宽广，各地风土人情差别很大，充满了吸引力。在深圳的两年间，他游玩了中国许多地方，最喜欢的就是阳朔、长沙、广州三个城市。阳朔是中国广西壮族自治区的一个县城，拥有美丽的漓江山水；长沙是中国湖南省的省会，历史悠久、文化丰富，拥有马王堆汉墓、岳麓书院等历史遗迹；广州是中国广东省的省会，经济繁荣、鲜花锦簇、美食诱人，也是世界上两千多年来长盛不衰的港口城市。亚当最喜欢的这三个城市风情各异，但都开放而自信地欢迎着各地游客。在中国深圳，对亚当来说，出国旅游尤其是去南亚和东南亚旅游也是非常方便的。短短两年多的时间，亚当去过印度、斯里兰卡、菲律宾、马来西亚、印度尼西亚、柬埔寨等国家。中国是他寻找精彩生活的目的地，也是他继续探索周边精彩地域的出发点。

亚当非常激动地谈到了在这里生活的方便和精彩。亚当和许多初来中国的外国朋友一样，对于智能手机拥有非常强大的功能表示惊叹。亚当感慨："在中国，智能手机的功能非常强大，几乎可以用手机做任何事情。如果你需要什么，总有一个软件可以帮你解决。"亚当喜欢使用微信和朋友们聊天，使用淘宝网在网上购物（送货的速度非常快），交房租也会用到手机软件。出门坐公交或者地铁时，他不再需要带上现金或者交通卡，只需要打开相应的手机软件刷一刷就能乘车了。最令亚当激动的是，当他初来深圳一切都很陌生时，是网络帮助他打开人际交往的大门，寻找到陪伴自己的女朋友——盖尔。他和盖尔在一款手机软件上聊起天，约见面后互相一见钟情，可以用中国古话说"千里

姻缘一线牵”。如今，亚当和盖尔在一起已经两年了。他们互相鼓励，彼此支持，甚至还一起养了一只睡觉像小猪一样打呼噜的小狗贝拉。亚当在中国生活的方便、精彩和结缘正是中国互联网飞速发展二十多年的科技创新带给普通人快乐生活的写照。在这里，每个人都能有机会享受创新社会带来的快乐。

为了记录下自己在深圳的精彩生活，亚当很快像全世界所有的年轻人一样用短视频的方式拍摄视频发布到网站上。他和女朋友一起尝试中文rap视频、中国旅游vlog、仿妆视频，等等。中国短视频业务发展迅猛，

在中国的亚当很快被相关的公司、节目组发现，得到了非常特别的机会。Papitube（中国最受欢迎的网络红人papi酱和团队创办的短视频机构）邀请亚当去了香港邮轮参加视频博主的活动，也邀请他参加了在北京拍视频的活动。亚当通过网络和短视频和中国最优秀的一批短视频制作者有了往来。除此之外，亚当还获得了“快乐大本营”的邀请，和许多中国家喻户晓的明星一起在电视节目上唱歌玩游戏。快乐大本营在中国已经连续播出了23年，并且是中国最受欢迎的综艺节目和收视率最高的综艺节目之一。作为一个普通人，亚当从未想过自己在这个国家可以活得如此刺激又出彩，能够被这么多中国人看到。这是亚当以前从未想到过的精彩生活。

亚当认为："这些经历都非常精彩。两年前我绝对没有想过我会经历这些。我喜欢在中国的每一天，我根本还没有想要去其他国家。"每一个读完亚当的故事的人都相信，他的中国故事还在继续，未来一定会更精彩。

Scan for a Video

出版策划：王君校　韩　晖
统筹协调：付　眉　韩　颖　彭　博
策划编辑：张　超
责任编辑：杨　晗
英文翻译：薛彧威　卢　敏　韩芙芸
英文编辑：韩芙芸
封面设计：智玖拾（成都）文化传媒有限公司
排　　版：北京几何创想艺术设计有限公司
印刷监制：汪　洋

图书在版编目（CIP）数据
第三只眼看中国．发现中国之美：汉英 / 王新玲主编．-- 北京：华语教学出版社，2021.3
ISBN 978-7-5138-2081-3

Ⅰ．①第… Ⅱ．①王… ②杨… Ⅲ．①新闻—作品集—中国—当代—汉英 Ⅳ．① I253

中国版本图书馆 CIP 数据核字 (2021) 第 035018 号

第三只眼看中国：发现中国之美

王新玲 主编

*

华语教学出版社有限责任公司出版
（中国北京百万庄大街 24 号　邮政编码 100037）
电话：(86)10-68320585, 68997826
传真：(86)10-68997826, 68326333
网址：www.sinolingua.com.cn
电子信箱：hyjx@sinolingua.com.cn
北京虎彩文化传播有限公司印刷
2021 年（16 开）第 1 版
2022 年第 1 版第 2 次印刷
（汉英）
ISBN 978-7-5138-2081-3
009800